Bullet Bungalow

THE STALKER

--- PULLING THREADS ---

Book One

SHERYLL O'BRIEN

This is a work of fiction. All characters in this book are the product of an overactive imagination. Any businesses, organizations, places, events, and incidents are used fictionally. Any resemblance to a real person, living or dead, is a tremendous coincidence.

ISBN 978-1-939351-12-8

WOODWIND PRESS

Printed in United States of America

To my mother, Ruth Shirley Bodreau.

Thank you for not saying – to my face –
everything you surely must be thinking.

I love you mieces to pieces –
whatever the hell that means.

ACKNOWLEDGMENT

I want to start by thanking my husband. Perhaps want is too strong a word, so I'll go with – I should start by thanking my husband.

Mr. Wonderful, it's hard to imagine that anyone else would have had the staying power with me. I feel compelled to remind you, in print, for all the world to see – should anything suspicious happen to me, no one will believe it was an accident.

I love you, Tim.

A heartfelt thank you to my team:

Andria Flores ~ Editor extraordinaire.
Nancy Pendleton ~ Goddess of the publishing world.
Jessica Champion ~ Web designer and manager.
25 Hours Consulting
Daryl Bruinsma ~ Cover Design & Animation.

Testimonials

"One book will set the hook!" ~ Nancy Pendleton

"This avid reader predicts that Sheryll O'Brien will become your favorite author. She's mine." ~ Ruth S. Bodreau

"The characters draw you in immediately. You will worry, laugh, hope, and love right along with them." ~ Donna Eaton

"There is nothing sweeter than a Sunday morning coffee, a blanket, overcast skies, and a *Pulling Threads* novel." ~ Andria Flores

"Everything you'd want in a good book. Humor, romance, suspense and great characters! It even takes place by the ocean! Loved it." ~ Helena Green

"I could write a book about the wonderfulness of it all." ~ Faith

"Hunks, humor, and heartache! What more could you ask for?" ~ Marjorie McCarthy

"*Bullet Bungalow* is a page turning family saga and then *Netti Barn* and *Cutters Cove* come along and add a whole lot of trauma to the drama." ~ Jessica O'Brien

"The most promising new author I've encountered in my publishing career!" ~ Jim P. - Woodwind Press

--- Pulling Threads ---

Bullet Bungalow
Netti Barn
Cutters Cove
They Run
They Hide
They Choose

Coming soon…

PENOBSCOT BAY
A Rocco Fiancetti Incorporated Investigation

Reasons
Rescues
Resolutions
Torment
Tango
Tests
Resolve
Revenge
Rebound

--- Twisted Threads ---

Coming soon…

Her Scream
Stay Safe

It all began.
Yesteryear

Maria and Patrick Mahoney worked at the summer home of wealthy industrialist, Alexander Eaton, in Laurel Falls, Massachusetts. By summer home, it should be noted that the Eaton place was like the mansions along the cliffs of Newport, grand estates with beautifully kept grounds and fiercely kept secrets.

Maria, a squat woman with tree-stump legs, thumped about the kitchen. She stirred this, cleaned that, and muttered in a language that was of her own making. Part of "Maria-speak" came from her native Italian, part from her husband's native Gaelic, and part from her easily enraged and foul-mouthed employer. A domestic in the Eaton estate, Maria was always short on time and temper when her husband came in for lunch. "Patrick, damn mangia, cheana," she demanded.

Patrick took the cheese sandwich from a chipped china plate she pushed his way, grabbed an apple, and kissed his squat woman atop her head before escaping the heat of Maria's kitchen and Maria's ire. A stone mason, Patrick moved to the far end of a wall he was extending and sat amid the tall grass of a windswept dune. He watched his employer walk the wet packed sand near the ocean's edge, dressed in a white button shirt cuffed to the elbow, trousers tucked into gentlemen's socks, and a pair of spit-polished Florsheims. Patrick shook his head at the man. "Damn fool," he muttered, using one of his employer's favorite sayings.

Alexander Eaton dressed for what he was, an exceedingly wealthy man who came by his initial wealth the old-fashioned way—he inherited it. Then he parlayed his fortune tenfold. "Radio, television, movie production—that's where the money and the fun are," he told his associates and the lovely ladies that draped his arms. In early 1927, the wealthy industrialist told his domestic and stone mason, "I am deeding a parcel of land on the far edge of my property to you." The husband and wife offered small smiles as they clasped hands. Uproariously, Eaton insisted, "This parcel is not for you to keep. It is for me. The deed is temporary, and the land will be reversed to me if times become tough." Two short years later, times became tough for Alexander Eaton. "It's crashed? It's gone?" The no-longer-wealthy, and oh-so-despondent industrialist retired to his study one evening, took a silver revolver from his desk, and put a bullet through his head.

"O Signore!" Maria cried at the gruesome sight. Her trembling hands flourished the sign of the cross, then found her wetting cheeks. Patrick moved past his wife into the room, went to the desk upon which his deceased employer was sprawled, and took from within the deed that granted the domestic and the stone mason ownership of two acres of beachfront property in Laurel Falls. He folded the deed, took hold of his squat woman's hand, and walked out the front door muttering a final, "Damn fool."

Bullet Bungalow

One giant hopscotch jump.

Kitt Mahoney is doing the two best things in the world—her world anyway. She is watching her daughters enjoy the last rays and days of summer, and she is taking in the sights and sounds of *her* ocean—the one at Laurel Falls, Massachusetts. The Atlantic doesn't belong to Kitt, of course, but it does play with the shoreline she now owns. From as far back as she can remember, Kitt has loved the ocean at Laurel Falls. Having grown up in neighboring Mayflower, the native New Englander has always had sand, surf, and sea in her life, but she swears that the ocean in Mayflower is different than the ocean in Laurel Falls.

Kitt's oldest daughter, Annie, a poodle-sized young woman with a pit bull-sized mouth has particularly strong opinions on this subject, and she has expressed her opinion. Often.

"Mom, of all the hairbrained theories you've come up with, this is the whopper. The Atlantic Ocean in Mayflower is the same Atlantic Ocean in Laurel

Falls. In fact, I can prove that point with a float, some waves, and an undertow."

It's usually at that point in their back and forth that the daughter is handed a float, along with a bit of attitude from her mother, "Have at it, Miss Mahoney-Maxwell."

Kitt recently came to own the Laurel Falls property through a forgotten deed, land hand-me-downs, and one giant hopscotch jump. Her great-great-grandparents, Patrick and Maria Mahoney, were sort of deeded a two-acre section of land from wealthy industrialist, Alexander Eaton, who sort of forgot about the transaction. On a particularly bad day in 1929, the absentminded man crashed headfirst into a speeding bullet leaving the *sort of deeded land* to the Mahoney's. The couple never took kindly to their fortune being changed by a bullet to a man's head, so they left the land untouched. Subsequent Mahoney generations were less squeamish about the circumstances of land hand-me-downs. As each generation inherited the oceanfront property, they did *something* to leave their mark. Terrence Mahoney, Kitt's great-grandpa, built stone walls along the property line with twin stone arches at either end. Her grandparents, Joseph and Kathleen, built a modest bungalow with a beautiful double-sided stone fireplace as their *something*. Next in line for the land hand-me-down was Kitt's father, James, but that's when the great hopscotch jump occurred.

Kitt opened the packet her grandfather handed her, and removed several documents. "Grandpa, you left Laurel Falls to me?" He nodded, "Kittridge…" The only man brave enough to call her that began, "…there is nothing more sacred to an Irishman than his land…" Kitt could have finished her grandpa's story about the potato famine since she'd heard it as often as she'd repeated the childhood ditty—one potato, two potato, three potato, four—but, it was never wise to interrupt Joseph Mahoney, so she remained silent. "…the Mahoney family left their Ireland because of *Gorta Mór,* the Great Hunger, where millions died without a morsel in their mouths, land of their own beneath their feet, or prayers within their souls." Her grandpa would always finish his life lessons with… "God, family, and land, the Irishman's trinity."

Like generations before, Kitt took land ownership seriously. She decided that her *something* was going to be a major renovation and expansion of the bungalow. The grueling construction project nearly caused the woman to end it with a bullet to the head, *à la* Moneybags. Throughout the yearlong project she complained incessantly. "What is it with these

Neanderthals? Does not even one of them own a belt? Hard hats and ass cracks as far as the eye can see. I tell you; the construction business is a scourge. And don't even get me started on..."

It was usually at that point that the eyes of her listener would glaze and an exasperated sigh would be heard—the exasperated sigh came from Kitt. When construction was finally finished, the elated woman invited those who were still speaking to her to a day of picnicking and swimming at Laurel Falls. As the wonderful day of seaside frivolity came to a close, Kittridge Anne Mahoney dedicated her place with a most irreverent tip of the hat to Moneybags. "Please join me in a toast to Alexander Eaton and his last great deed, pun intended. I christen my oceanfront home, Bullet Bungalow."

As she sipped a glass of champagne on the porch of her home, she had a vision of her great-great-grandmother flourishing the sign of the cross with a fearful, "O Signore!" and her great-great-grandfather murmuring, "Damn fool." Kitt laughed away the thoughts of relatives she never knew, and took in the sights and sounds of *her* ocean and fell in love, all over again.

It was all good.

"Mom. Earth to Mom!"

Kitt snaps to attention as Callie and Tess bounce before her, teeth chattering and dripping from head to toe. "Good Lord, girls where are your towels?"

"Annie took them," they cry in unison.

The girls are referring to their 21-year-old, sun-worshiping sister, Annie Mahoney-Maxwell. The pixie-sized woman is a force to be reckoned with, and her two younger sisters are currently reckoning with her. "I gave them fair warning that I'd take their towels if they kept blocking the sun," she casually calls up from the lawn.

The mother raises a brow at the shivering girls, "Well, you were warned," she says as she hands each girl a toasty warm, just-out-of-the-dryer towel. Callie and Tess quaver their thanks and plop onto the porch sofa. Although born to different mothers, the 14-year-old girls are always mistaken as twins. They have long, wavy, honey-blonde hair and vivid blue eyes. Callie's have a tad more aqua in hers, and Tess has a tiny dimple under her left eye that no one but Kitt tends to notice. If not for those differences they're identical.

"Kitt. Earth to Kitt!"

Once again, she snaps to attention. This time, she is stirred by John Maxwell who is bounding up the porch stairs and calling her name. Choruses of "Dad" ring out from his three girls, who haven't seen him in four long weeks. Each year, John leaves for the month of August on a combined business-vacation trip. Each year, Kitt teases that he meets a mysterious lover for a secret rendezvous, to which he always replies, "Kitt, if I was with another woman, would I be sending 'wish you were here' postcards?" He nudges, she laughs.

"Hey, John," she casually says, "I heard you were back—actually, I heard you were back days ago," she pries.

"Aaron Rodgers must be in town," he shrugs his broad shoulders and smirks. Before his smirk fades, he is swarmed by his girls and shares hugs and kisses all around. Kitt's hug comes last and sans a kiss.

"Mmm," she murmurs.

"Mmm, what?" he asks as a strand of her hair whips across his face courtesy of a lifting ocean breeze.

"Mmm, no kiss for the mother of your children? Perhaps you're all kissed out from your yearly fling? It was Madrid this year, right?"

John's almost smile quickly fades. "No fling," he snarls.

With or without his trademark smirk or occasional snarl, the father of Kitt's children is very good looking. He has medium-brown hair, and aqua blue eyes that are easily readable one minute and mysteriously hooded the next. A doppelganger of Green Bay Packers quarterback, Aaron Rodgers, he is tall, lean, and muscular. In a nutshell John Maxwell is everything a girl could want—Kitt Mahoney wanted him twice upon a time.

John and Kitt were the "it" couple going into their senior year at Mayflower-Falls Regional High School. They had it all—good looks, good grades, and the promise of a good future. They also had one too many good times in the back seat of Mr. Maxwell's Ford Bronco. "I'm pregnant." Kitt told her steady beau at the Homecoming Dance. John didn't smirk, he just held her close. The following spring, they became parents to Annie. "What do we do with *it?*" John asked for the fourth time in that many minutes while peering through the nursery room glass at their tiny bundle wrapped in pink. "*Her.*" Kitt reminded him for the fourth time while standing on wobbly legs from a birthing experience she was neither prepared for nor terribly brave about. The young parents quickly learned that what they do with "it – her," is whatever "it – she," wanted.

During Annie's first year, John and Kitt learned how to care for a child. "She needs to be changed." How to share responsibilities. "It's your turn." And how to lean on one another. "I need to pee, so watch her." During the toughest times, they would clasp hands and affirm that they were partners and always would be. Of course, half of the partnership got to go home to his parents' house, leaving Annie with Kitt 24/7.

"God, Mom! Where do you keep going?" Annie scoffs from no more than two feet from where Kitt is standing.

"I'm right here, Annie."

"Okay, tell me what Callie just said."

"I think you mean, 'tell me what Callie just asked' because she asked if she and Tess can stay another night at the bungalow."

John leans in and whispers, "Cheater. You know Callie always asks that."

Kitt blows an air kiss to ward off Annie's eye daggers, smiles conspiratorially at John, and nods her approval to Callie and Tess. They squeal their delight and dance around, while Annie, John and Kitt set the porch table for dinner. After burgers, corn-on-the-cob, and salad, Annie heads to her newly renovated mini master off the living room while the parents trek upstairs with the younger girls for goodnight hugs.

"Do you feel like hanging out a while?" Kitt asks before John makes the hasty retreat, she can tell he's thinking about.

He shakes his head, "Can't. I've got a ton of work at Netti Barn." He gives her the kiss he held back earlier then moves toward the porch.

"You've been gone a month," she tries once again.

"That's why I need to get to Netti," he dismisses her once again.

Netti Barn is John's software design company—it's the name of it and the location of it. Within days of Tess and Callie's births, John bought the property on the outskirts of Mayflower for the Mahoney-Maxwell clan. The farmland spread, once owned by the Netti family, came with a pale yellow, two-story farmhouse, matching two-story barn, and fourteen gorgeous acres of land sectioned from an original hundred-acre parcel. John fell into ownership of the property the day Daniel Netti put it on the market. "There's a lot of interest in the place, John. Are you sure you can swing it? I don't want to miss out on other offers," Daniel explained.

Kitt would have asked the same question had Daniel not beaten her to it. She was still in questioning mode long after John shook Daniel's hand and affirmed. "I can swing it."

Kitt had no idea how John was financing the place, and he wasn't saying. Apparently, the enormity of the whole thing gave her a serious case of heartburn—the burn part settling on her face. "Kitt, don't worry, I have it all planned. We'll all live in the farmhouse. I'll work in the barn, you'll work at the college, and the kids will grow up at Netti. It's all good."

It was all good.

Nobody. Ever. Mentions.

"What are you thinking about?" Annie startles Kitt from behind when she enters the kitchen.

"Will you please stop sneaking up on me?"

"Just walking through, Mom," Annie says as she heads to the porch and parks herself on the sofa.

Kitt grabs a glass of Moscato, pulls on a black and white Baja hoodie and joins her daughter. Annie looks at her mother's new garment and rolls her eyes. "Kinda old for a drug rug, don't you think?" she cuts with her acerbic tongue.

Kitt perches on the open corner of the couch, tucks her feet beneath her thighs, and swats her daughter's hand away from her wine glass, "Go get your own."

"Don't want any, just want to bug you," she smirks.

Kitt's oldest daughter and her father are thicker than thieves and share many qualities and abilities. Smirks are most definitely at the top of the list of things they share.

"You never answered my question," Annie nudges.

"What question?"

"What were you thinking about when I startled you?"

"Netti," the word escapes on a sigh.

Annie sighs in response. It's a nice sigh, the kind of sigh that wraps warm memories. They sit in silence, the rhythmic sounds of the ocean keeping them company. Kitt doesn't know where Annie's thoughts go, but Kitt's take her back to Netti.

As soon as John closed on the property, the Mahoney-Maxwell clan moved into the farmhouse. Annie, Callie, and Kitt lived on the second floor and Tess and John on the first. There were no doors separating the upstairs from the downstairs, so the girls came and went at will between them. "Where's Callie?" Kitt would ask. "With Dad," the kids would answer. "Where's Tess?" she'd ask. "With Callie," they'd answer. "Where's Annie?" she'd ask. "Who cares?" they'd answer, then laugh until their sides hurt. The three girls were raised as sisters and are siblings in every way possible. Although Tess isn't Kitt's daughter by birth, they love each other just the same.

For a dozen years, the clan lived in the two-story farmhouse, John ran his business out of the barn, and the kids raised all kinds of hell at Netti. When Kitt inherited the beachfront bungalow in neighboring Laurel Falls, a short eleven miles away, Annie moved there with Kitt. The move was done piecemeal throughout the yearlong renovation project. "The porch is done.

We can put the table and chairs there and have a few meals," Kitt called out and they'd celebrate with a few meals there. "Hey, Annie, I got the go-ahead to move things into your mini master," which sent Annie packing and John and Kitt schlepping. "Tess, you are not having pink and white chevron wallpaper—Callie you are not having aqua and white polka dot wallpaper." The mother threatened.

When Annie and Kitt were fully relocated, they began their new lives at Bullet Bungalow. The two of them commute from Laurel Falls to Littleton College where Annie is a senior and where Kitt works. Callie and Tess live at the farm with John during the school year and join their sister and mother at the beach on weekends and all summer long.

"Hey, Mom..." Annie pauses. Annie never pauses. Annie pushes.

Kitt turns toward her daughter, giving her undivided attention, which is no easy feat since the ocean is vying strongly for Kitt's undivided attention. "What?" she asks, then waits through a bit more pausing.

"I've been thinking about Joy."

Those five words cause Kitt's brain to come to a **screeching halt**. Joy Ann Watts is the former love of John Maxwell, the mother of Tess, and the person who nobody ever mentions. Nobody. Ever. Mentions.

"Why?" the stunned woman asks in a tone of voice that one is most likely to hear in a horror flick.

"No clue, but she's been looping through my head for days."

"Well, get her out!"

Annie laughs, "I know the basics about the 'Joy Saga'. There's more, right?"

"Tons."

"Well…" she prompts.

"Now? You want to talk about Joy, now?" Kitt astonishes as she bangs her brains inside her shaking head.

"Got something else to do?" Annie raises a quizzical brow.

Kitt hands her daughter an empty wine glass, "Better fill this up and get one for yourself."

They had condoms back then.

Kitt quickly gathers her thoughts, the ones she hasn't gathered in years.

A year after Annie's birth, John headed to UMass Amherst and Kitt commuted to Littleton College, a private liberal arts school on the North Shore, overlooking the Atlantic Ocean. They were no longer a couple, just co-parenting friends starting separate lives at separate schools. Sort of. John came home every Friday to be with Annie and would take her next door to his parents for the weekend. On the way out, with their pink bundle in tow, he'd say, "I've got this Kitt, go out, do your own thing, hang out with Maura." The young mother did that on occasion, but she mostly stayed in studying, and would eventually place "the call". She didn't have to say anything. John said it all…"Do you want to come over? Annie's asleep. We can watch a movie or something." They knew full well what "something" meant, and they full well did "something" on many, many occasions.

Kitt is just about to trip down memory lane and land face first in a sex memory about John when Annie returns with two glasses and a new bottle of effervescent yumminess. Kitt raises a quizzical brow, "Rather ambitious."

"It's a two-for. One, it will dull any pain or anxiety this conversation might cause you. And two, if I ply you with enough of it, you're less likely to hedge or sugarcoat stuff."

"Well played," she raises her glass in salute. "And the Beatles tunes in the background?"

"Again, a two-for. One, if Callie or Tess come down, they'll sing along with whatever song is on, so we'll hear them and can stop talking. And two, I figured you might appreciate the soundtrack of your life playing in the background as you're reliving it."

"Annie, I'm in my thirties. Beatles tunes are not the soundtrack of my life," she chuckles.

"Late thirties. And since they're on steady loop around here I guess they're the soundtrack of my life," she laughs, then sips. "Okay, spill."

Kitt takes a fortifying gulp knowing full well this is a thread she should not pull. "Okay, you know that your father met Joy his senior year at UMass. Well, they became…" the mother looks at her daughter, her grown daughter, yes, but her daughter, nonetheless. Annie's eyes are rapt and drilling with expectation. "Nope, nope, can't." Kitt shakes her brain around a bit more.

Annie nudges her mother's hand toward her lips, "Drink. Pretend I'm Maura, even though I don't have her boobs."

Kitt laughs and spits the sip she just took all over her startled daughter.

Annie laughs and wipes the spittle away, "Now you owe me. Spill, don't spit."

The reluctant woman pulls a long breath and goes for it. "When your father met Joy, they became hot and heavy really fast. He brought her to meet you and me on one of his weekend visits home, and they spent Christmas break at the Maxwell's. The four of us were together almost every minute. I think your father wanted to see how we would all get on."

"Joy was nice and pretty." Annie catches herself and raises her glass, "I don't know where that came from, but I guess the bubbly is working on me, too."

"You remember Joy?" Kitt asks with a quizzical, raised brow.

"I found a picture of her in a box in your walk-in. She looks like Amanda Seyfried."

"Yup, they're doppelgangers. Well, back to the saga. After Christmas, you and I never saw Joy again. The two of them went back for spring semester and dropped off the face of the earth."

"I remember that, too," Annie says sadly.

Tears sting Kitt's eyes. She suddenly remembers how much Annie missed her father during his disappearing act. "I think we have a bad bottle of Moscato, and it's putting us into a funk. Let's pick up this conversation another time," the mother tries.

"Just get me to the part where I ended up with doppelganger sisters from non-doppelganger mothers," the daughter pushes.

"Oh, that."

"Yes, *that*," Annie mocks.

"Your father and Joy broke up at graduation. He came home that night for a joint graduation party our parents planned for us. He didn't bring Joy, and he didn't say why." Kitt pauses, she sips, she hopes poodle-Annie becomes drowsy. What she gets instead is an energized pit bull-Annie.

"And what? You got drunk on Moscato and got pregnant with Callie?"

"Tequila."

Annie shakes her head, "They had condoms back then, and birth control pills, you know."

"I'm aware."

Annie shakes her head and mumbles in a most derisive tone, "Parents."

"Are you done judging?" the disparaged parent asks in a most annoyed tone.

"Probably not, but continue," Annie raises her glass in another salute.

"Your father and Joy reconciled in a matter of days and..."

"*Tess*," Annie offers in exasperation.

"Tess what?" Kitt's 14-year-old daughter, Callie, sings from the kitchen in tune with *Hey*

Jude that's currently playing on the soundtrack of her mother's life.

Annie shoots wide eyes Kitt's way. The mom goes into mom-mode, which is where she should have stayed all along. "Callie, please don't pick up Annie's bad habit of sneaking up on people."

"Not sneaking, Mom, just came down for waters. You never answered my question, Tess what?"

Annie uses her pit bull mouth to deflect and disarm, "I asked Mom who she likes better, you or Tess. Mom chose Tess. I repeated it because I was a little surprised. You're way better than Tess," the lying little dog says as she gathers the wine bottle and glasses.

"Annie," Kitt admonishes in her best mom-tone, but is silently applauding her daughter's quick wit. "You did not ask that question."

"Did so," Annie laughs as she pulls Callie through the kitchen and living room. Their voices fade as one heads to her mini master and the other to her aqua and white polka dot bedroom upstairs.

Kitt stays on the porch for a few minutes letting *her* ocean lull what's left of her senses. She must have dozed off because she wakes with a start. The hair on her arms and neck prickle; her head reflexively turns toward the woods that abut the driveway and side yard. *Footfalls?* She holds her breath and leans into the direction of the sound. Nothing. Still, her hair is standing on end and her spine is tingling. Kitt's fight or flight instinct kicks in. She flies into the house, slams the door, and locks it behind her.

THE STALKER

A man in a black hoodie steps from the tree line. "Goodnight, Kitt."

Hard hats and ass cracks.

Annie and Kitt head separately to Littleton College; Annie to begin her senior year, and Kitt to begin what feels like her hundredth. In order to fulfill an undergraduate work study requirement nearly two decades ago, Kitt did clerical work in Littleton's development office. After rising through the ranks and earning her Master in Institutional Advancement, she now leads the College's dynamic fundraising team. As she crosses the quad, she is met with friendly greetings and happy banter.

"Hi, Kitt."

"Nice to see you, Kitt."

"Back for another year, Kitt? What's this your twentieth?"

She laughs and answers, "Nope. My hundredth."

Even the grumpy Sergeant Cluster offers a welcome back smile. It doesn't reach his eyes, but it's more than she usually gets.

Kitt's back to school excitement is immediately quashed by the sounds of whirling saws, banging hammers, and rat-a-tat-tatting nail guns. Her heart sinks when she realizes the wretched sounds of construction are coming from inside the Administrative building where her office is located. She is suddenly reminded of that movie where the terrified babysitter learns that the stalker's phone calls are coming from inside the house. The exasperated woman groans because it's clear that the construction noise is coming from inside her building.

"I'd rather have a stalker."

Panic rises as she navigates the halls. A throng of hard hats and ass cracks suddenly appear from nowhere like tormenters in an amusement park Fun House. Her breathing and pulse quicken, a fine layer of sweat forms along her brow and lip. "Good Lord, get hold of yourself," she quietly admonishes. "I know, I'll sing. Lions and tigers and bears, oh my...lions and tigers and bears, oh my...hammers and saws and sweat. Oh my God! I'm losing it." She scurries around workers, nearly taking out two as she increases her pace. "I think I recognize that hard hat, but without his ass crack who knows for sure. Oh my God! I have PTSD!" Desperation trumps decorum. She runs the rest of the way, and throws herself into her office. "What the hell is wrong with those men? Do they not feel a breeze along the cracks of their asses? Is there some sort of construction rule that states, 'when you lift your hammer you must drop your drawers?'"

Jane Harper, Kitt's Southern belle assistant raises a debutant's brow, holds out a set of earplugs and drawls, "Use these."

Kitt raises a non-debutant's brow in return, "Shielding me from the construction noise? Or you, from my construction-bitching? Matters not, I suppose."

The sufficiently ear-plugged woman spends the rest of the day behind closed doors, and when she finally ventures out of her office, the halls are quiet and ass crack free. She pushes through the front door, practically skips across the parking lot, tosses a goodbye wave to the sergeant who is also making his way across campus, rides home with all four windows down, the sunroof open, and Beatles tunes blaring. She is loving the feel of sun on her face, and the dance of her hair as it blows in all directions. As she turns off Farmington, onto Tarrington, she sees Annie pulling her Jeep onto the bungalow's driveway with Kitt's RAV4 in hot pursuit. They bound from their cars, and race one another to the porch, where Kitt returns once she's changed into shorts and a tee. John and the girls arrive minutes later in a flurry of laughter, with pizza boxes and soda bottles in hand. Kitt pulls away when he goes to kiss her hello.

"What, no kiss?" he asks. "Did you have a bad day?"

"Did you forget last night?" The whole ritual of kissing when they greet is weird on some level, but John Maxwell and Kitt Mahoney have known one another for decades. They have been friends for all that time, lovers for some of that time, and co-parents for a big swath of that time. They are family, and their families greet one another with a kiss—except for Annie because one never knows if you'll get the poodle or the pit bull.

The Mahoney-Maxwell clan quickly grab seats around the table and jump in with first-day-of-school stories. Whoever isn't food chewing, is word spewing. "...and then my locker wouldn't lock," Callie says.

"They put me in French, and I wanted Spanish," Tess complains.

"I wanted French, and they put me in Spanish," Callie counter-complains.

"Curse of the doppelgangers," they say in unison.

If John's and Annie's thing is their smirk, then the girls' thing is talking in unison. The sister doppelgangers have a twin thing, and saying the same thing at the same time is their twin thing. "Coach Lemire, said, 'see you at tryouts,'" they say.

"When are tryouts?" John asks.

"Two weeks," they answer.

Kitt swallows her pizza and jumps into the fray, "There's a construction crew in my building." Those words bring the conversation to a **screeching halt**. Silent looks ricochet like errant Ping-Pong balls amongst her tablemates.

John breaks the silence, "Well that explains the no kiss greeting."

"Yours or mine?" she challenges.

"Touché," he raises his can of soda.

She turns to her firstborn, "You're awfully quiet." She touches Annie's arm, "Is something bothering you?"

She nods, "I don't know what. Just a nudge that something isn't right, you know?"

Kitt is reminded of the feeling she had the night before, the one that sent her hurtling through the kitchen door, "I hate those kinds of nudges." A shiver runs her spine, and her arms goose bump at the memory.

After dinner, John starts wrapping leftover pizza slices for school lunches. Kitt cranks the tunes—Beatles tunes—they play on a near continuous loop in her house. Apparently, they play even when she's not home. Kitt is very good about turning off all things electrical before she heads out, one might say that she is obsessive about it. Even so, she and Annie were welcomed home by The Beatles, that afternoon.

"Did you come home during the day?" Kitt called out to Annie after their race in from the driveway.

"Nope. Why?"

"I'm sure I turned the tunes off before I left this morning."

"Maybe Dad stopped by."

Kitt laughed, "If that were the case, we'd have been greeted by the brothers Allman or Doobie."

Before Kitt can ask John if he stopped by earlier, the parents find themselves encircled by their pack of screaming meemies—who are screaming the lyrics to *Maxwell's Silver Hammer*. John Maxwell plays along, pretending to hammer Kitt's head. She plays along, pretending to collapse dead in his arms. It is an old routine. Fits of laughter follow the girls as they head to the living room.

John continues his playacting and moves menacingly toward Kitt. In his scary voice, he whispers in her ear. "Better not be alone with Maxwell."

She feigns horror, "You have no intention of killing me do you, Maxwell?"

"Not tonight, Ms. Mahoney. My silver hammer is in the shop."

Goosebumps raise at John's menacingly-delivered words. She rubs her arms, then points to an array of Moscato bottles that line her countertop. "One of those might work."

"If I want you out cold, all I have to do is ply you with what's in the bottle, not hit you with the bottle," he says as he dips her.

"You're in a better mood," she hip-chucks him.

"I am," he hip-chucks her. "Sorry about last night," he says with a kiss to her temple.

"All's forgiven."

Before you say no.

John takes Callie and Tess to Netti Farmhouse shortly before nine. Not quite ready to head to her home office, Kitt sits out on her back porch and communes with her ocean. She is blissfully headed toward mellow when a memory of, "the woman who nobody ever mentions" pushes in.

"Hey, Annie, your dad and Joy are here."

The little imp with waist-length hair and big round eyes came running into the room, "Daddy! Daddy! Joy! Joy!" John scooped his girl into his arms. Joy offered a smile—it was not the wide smile Kitt remembered her having the last time they were all together. Halfway through the hour visit, Kitt pulled John aside, "What the hell is up with Joy? Are you two fighting?"

"No."

"Did I do something to piss her off?"

"No."

"Is she on drugs?"

"No."

Kitt changed course. "Forget Joy. What the hell is up with you?"

"We're leaving."

"John! You need to spend time with Annie. Alone time. And don't bring Joy back here unless she's fun Joy."

Kitt is pulled from her head-banging visit with "hostile Joy" by the crunch of driveway gravel. A minute later she hears a muffled...

"Hey Kitt, you there?" Seconds later, Maura Putnam, Kitt's BFF since preschool pokes her head around the corner. Kitt is pleased as punch to see Maura—until she sees her shit-eating grin.

"Maura. Why are you smiling like that?" she asks. Before she gets another word out, Maura bounds up the stairs. Kitt has a fraction of a second to shield herself before her Best Flying Friend goes airborne, lands with a thud onto the sofa, and snuggles her tight against its side. Kitt struggles to free herself—to no avail.

"Before you say no, hear me out," Maura pleads.

"No."

"Kitt, *pleeeeease!*"

Maura Putnam is an emergency room nurse practitioner at Mayflower-Falls Regional Medical Center. She is also the best friend a girl can have, although it is a challenge for Kitt being in the same room with Maura at times. A Jessica Rabbit lookalike, Maura is tall and sexy—Kitt is not and not. The only similarity between the women is their hair. It's long, luscious, and wavy.

Maura's is siren sexy red, Kitt's is acorn-brown, the same color as her eyes.

The BFF's stunning beauty and fun nature never leaves her wanting for a date. Some might say that Kitt's bestie is a tad on the fun side of easy, but truth be told, Maura considers dating a contact sport, and she will compete until she finds "the one". Until that day arrives, Kitt lives vicariously through Maura. She finds the experience both exhilarating and exhausting. There is one thing about Kitt's childhood friend that really pisses her off, she is always trying to fix her up with some doctor or other. No matter how resistant Kitt is to the gentle push, or the all-out pull, Maura is equally persistent, which is why the woman with acorn-brown eyes, and nutty-brown hair has been on countless dates over the years.

Apparently, Kitt has zoned out again because the next thing she hears is…

"…so it's not for you, Kitt, it's for me."

"What's for you?" she asks.

"The faux date," Maura groans. "Gosh, Kitt, weren't you even listening?"

"She never listens."

The women nearly jump out of their skins at the interruption. "Annie! How long have you been standing there?" Kitt demands.

"Long enough to conclude that you won't go on the date, even though you should."

"Annie, not that it's any of your business, but I'm too busy to date. Besides, nothing ever comes of it, anyway."

"The date isn't for you, Mom, it's for Auntie Maura. She's your friend, and friends do stuff for one another that they don't want to do." Turning to Maura, Annie adds, "Good luck getting her to budge." Then, as though swept into the ether, Annie disappears.

"God, I hate it when she does that," Kitt groans.

"Disappears?" Maura asks.

"Materializes," Kitt replies.

THE STALKER

He paces and grouses. "The daughters. The bastard father. The slutty redhead. They're always around. Why can't they leave her alone?"

He needs her to be alone. She was alone for a few minutes on the porch and he was enjoying the sight of her staring out at the darkened ocean sipping a glass of wine. He felt a small stirring down below when she licked the wine from her lips. He imagined the liquid as it slid down her throat. He thinks he might want to kiss her lips—or maybe cut her throat. He isn't sure yet.

Serves me right.

Maura gets the not-so-happy-double-dater at 7 PM. "Tell me about my faux date again," Kitt's words are practically swallowed by a yawn.

"For the love of all things holy, Kitt, liven up!"

"Maura. It's my first week back to work. I'm exhausted. John had to keep the girls another night. I don't want to go on a faux date. And I hate the word faux."

Maura sighs, "I told you, already. Steve and I need cover. That's where you and his new partner, Fred, come in. If anyone from the hospital sees Steve and me out together, I can just say that you and I were out and just happened to bump into the detectives."

Even though Maura explained the medical center's new non-fraternization policy between ER personnel and first-responders, Kitt still doesn't get it. "Maura. You're thirty-seven years old. Don't you think you're too old for this junior high crap?" she raises her hand to silence her friend. "Nope, don't answer me, just leave a note in my locker or have Jenny give it to me in homeroom."

Maura ignores her BFF's quip. Then, on the sweetest of sighs she whispers, "Kitt, I really like Steve."

Maura Putnam's confession surprises the hell out of Kitt Mahoney, and leaves her with only one thing to say. "Well, then, let the faux date begin."

Evviva Cucina
The Italian restaurant in Beverly, Massachusetts, is the perfect place for Kitt's first faux date. She's been to the restaurant many times, and really likes the rustic and laidback feel of the place. The layout lends itself to easy conversation and relaxed dining and if the atmosphere somehow fails to deliver, Evviva Cucina has a very interesting menu. It also has a very large bar at which two very buff, tremendously handsome men are standing. Kitt has no inkling which man is Maura's, but she is mentally cartwheeling for joy on her friend's behalf. Maura has no sooner chosen a table for two when the hunks appear by her side. Three of the foursome know one another so Kitt is quickly introduced to Steve and Fred, sans last names. Apparently, faux dates are conducted on a first-name-only basis. Within seconds, the guys enact "the plan" suggesting the gals join them for dinner.

The men sit across from the women giving Kitt a perfect view of Maura's heartthrob—so she views. Detective Steve Phelps could easily be described as cute-handsome. He's one of those guys who brings their childhood look into adulthood, slap a ball cap onto his head, a team jersey onto his back, and he's 7-year-old Stevie. The thirty-something year old man is clean-cut, has a permanently affixed smile, and playfully engaged eyes that are currently engaged on Maura. Unlike most men who notice Maura's ample Cs to the exclusion of all else, Steve's eyes never once stray from his date's extraordinary emeralds. "He's hooked," Kitt whispers. She takes a quick look at her BFF, "So's she," Kitt happily confirms. When she's had her fill of the happy twosome, she turns her attention to her faux date—the one who is staring—assessing? "What?" she snaps.

"Nothing. Just waiting," he calmly answers.

"For what?"

"For our faux date to begin," he says through a million-watt smile.

Returning his million-watter with one of her own, she replies, "Well, then, let the faux date begin, Fred........." there's a fill in the blank pause.

"Serpico," he immediately fills in the blank.

"Yeah, right. Detective Serpico?" she laughs.

He nods.

"Serpico?" she rolls her eyes.

He nods.

"Any relation to **the** Detective Frank Serpico of the NYPD?" she says with a mocking tone.

He nods.

"You're kidding. Right?"

He shrugs a shoulder. The detective's smile is so wide, it looks positively painful.

Kitt laughs again. "I'm sitting with Detective Fred Serpico, well isn't that just one for the books. I'm on a fake date and I haven't a clue if you're telling the truth. Serves me right."

Fred laughs big.

Kitt takes a minute to settle in, while she settles, she assesses. Fred Serpico, if that *is* his real name, is handsome. There's nothing boyish in his looks—he is all M.A.N. He has very nice, slightly wavy black hair and darkish eyes. His strong jaw is covered with a neatly trimmed scruff that barely hides the cleft in his chin. He has long, line dimples that cut his cheeks when he smiles, which so far is often. Kitts finds herself staring at the detective's hands, his rather large, undoubtedly strong hands. Hands that are currently holding a menu, *Lord, I wish they were holding my size Bs.* **Screech—faux date**, she quickly reminds herself.

"So, Kitt, have you decided?"

"The Pesto Chicken Caprese salad," she moans—a bit on the orgasmic side. A heady silence fills the space between the faux daters. She peeks over her menu. Fred is looking in her direction, his eyes are hooded, his mouth is in a sexy grin. "The salad is phenomenal," she sheepishly offers.

"Yeah, I got that from your moan. Make it two," he says to the waitress who smiles, takes their menus, and practically curtsies her chest into Fred's face.

Back off, Bimbo. **Screech—faux date**!

Once their food orders are in, Maura and Steve head to the bar to chat with someone from the hospital. They say it will look less shady if they head gossip off at the pass.

Fred scoffs when they leave.

"What?" Kitt asks.

"This isn't a faux date. It's a setup," the detective claims as he extends his long legs and crosses them at the ankles.

"But...but," she stammers.

"Trust me. We've been hustled," he says through another million-watt smile. Leaning in so as not to be overheard, Fred says, "Steve asked me to do the whole faux date thing to help him out with Maura. When I agreed, he started talking about you. How pretty you are—he understated that part by the way. How smart you are, how much you love to swim and run. It doesn't take a detective to figure this is a setup."

"No, I suppose it doesn't." When her brain catches up with her mouth she asks, "So why did you do it, you know, agree to the faux date thing?"

Fred shrugs. "I just moved back to the state. I thought I should help my new partner with his woman. And I love Italian food." A very wide grin dimples Fred's cheeks and sets his eyes aflame with mischief. "And, I have a plan."

Sheryll O'Brien

As though Maura senses the faux daters are talking about her, she turns and waves. Kitt sends her bestie a chipper wave and the biggest faux fucking smile, then leans toward Fred and says, "Do tell."

"I think we should…"

Faux, faux, date.

The Serpico-Mahoney faux date turns into a fabulous faux, faux, date courtesy of Fred's plan. Since Maura and Steve went to great lengths to trick the unsuspecting duo into a first date, then the conspirators are going to witness the hottest first date in history. If they were hoping to light a flicker between Fred and Kitt, then they are going to get a blowtorch. The faux couple pretend to get into the whole first date thing. They take turns asking questions—each one becoming more personal and intimate than the one before. They tune out the world, and tune in to each other.

"…I returned to Massachusetts after living in Washington State with my ex-wife, Veronica. We met at UMass Amherst and moved to Seattle after graduation."

Kitt rolls her eyes and groans.

He smiles, "Something wrong?"

"No. No. I just need to accept that everyone except me attended my dream school," she shrugs. "You were married a long time."

He nods, "After nearly twelve years of marriage and way too many years of undercover work, we eventually went our separate ways. Veronica got custody of the West Coast; I got custody of the East Coast. By the time we threw in the towel, it was almost too easy ending the marriage."

Kitt's thoughts turn to John.

Fred smiles, "You up for a little truth or dare of your own?"

She tells Fred about John, and Annie, and Callie, and Tess. About how she missed out on going to UMass, and how she's never left her alma mater, Littleton College. She is just about to tell Fred about the renovation project at Bullet Bungalow—which surprises her given how much she hated the renovation project at Bullet Bungalow—but as it turns out, Steve has beaten her to the punch. Fred tells her what he already knows and since he seems very interested in learning more, she tells him more.

"I pretty much gutted the place and extended the living space twenty by twenty feet."

"And that allowed for the mini master on the first floor."

"Yes. The mini is off the living room at the front of the house, and the master overlooks the ocean. Between them are twin, back to back bathrooms."

"How long were you under construction?"

"In people years or dog years? Because to me it's the same amount of time," she groans.

Fred laughs big.

As naturally as all get out, he reaches across the table and takes hold of her hand. She reminds herself that the gesture is nothing more than part of Fred's plan. Still, visions of his hands on her size Bs dance like sugarplums in her head. Two hours after their faux, faux, date began, Fred picks up the check and orders a Neapolitan crust Prosciutto and Fig pizza to go. His hand finds the small of her back as they walk out of Evviva Cucina—Kitt Mahoney's new favorite restaurant!

At Maura's car, Fred takes Kitt's hand and threads their fingers together. She swoons. The surprised woman can't tell if it is a real swoon, a faux swoon, or a faux, faux, swoon. But it is most definitely a swoon. Maura notices the hand holding and heart swooning and shoots Steve a glance that screams, "I told you so!"

Fred cuts off her silent gloating, "Hey, Steve. I'm sure Maura can give you a lift." With no further ado, Kitt's faux, faux, date puts his arm around her shoulder and leads her to his truck. She sends a big wave to Maura as she drives off with a detective named Serpico in his F-150, Bob Seger's *The Fire Down Below* blaring from the speakers.

But better.

"Seriously?"

"Seriously. I have never gone home after a night out with anyone other than Maura. She's got to be freaking out by now."

The faux daters sit for several minutes in Fred's truck, she can tell he is admiring the house and its setting. That's no surprise. Kitt's charming pale lavender bungalow with moss green shutters and ecru trim is nestled nicely between a stand of trees. It is the perfect place for some nursery rhyme character to stumble upon for a nap. Of course, the sweet little character would hightail it away when he or she came face to face with the pit bull pixie who lives inside.

Fred grabs the pizza and opens the driver's side door. A chuckle escapes her. "Fred, I think your pizza is safe in the truck."

"I think we should have a few slices before I leave," he casually explains when he opens her door.

"Why?"

"I'm starved. I would have ordered this pizza if you hadn't suggested the salad; it was moan-worthy by the way, but at the end of the day a salad is just a salad. Besides, Steve and Maura are gonna drive by."

"That's ridiculous," she laughs.

"They're gonna go get his Land Rover, it's less flashy than Maura's Caddie, and drive by to check if my truck is here. When they see that it is, they're gonna swing around, park nearby, and spy for a bit," he says with unwavering certainty.

Again, she laughs.

Fred takes hold of Kitt's hand and threads their fingers together. He gives it a little squeeze, "Steve is a detective, he's gonna check things out. And Maura's nosey, she's gonna make him check things out. I can leave now, but if I do there's really no shock effect. Remember, our goal for the faux, faux, date is to make it hot and make them wonder about us. If we end it now, it will be a win for them—we went to dinner, and I drove you home. Perfect end to our setup date. If you want to have a little more fun at their expense, I should stay awhile. Let them wonder what's going on inside the bungalow. Your call," he smiles.

"I'm in," she snickers.

Fred gently squeezes her hand, again. "Good, because they just drove by."

So far, the faux daters haven't disturbed Annie, and since Kitt would like to keep it that way, she takes Fred around back. They leave the pizza on the porch and head inside.

"Beautiful renovation. Who designed the layout?"

As they walk the first floor, she explains that she designed it according to her needs. "Two bedrooms up—two bedrooms down—bathrooms between the masters. I wanted to keep as much of the original kitchen as I could, but expand it a bit, so I incorporated part of the back porch as an extended work and dining area. The double-sided fireplace between the kitchen and living room is original, and my pride and joy. My grandpa built it," she says lovingly.

Fred stands for several minutes admiring the masonry. "It's beautiful. You don't need me to tell you that your grandpa was highly skilled, but he was. It would cost a fortune to have this built, today."

His eyes are moss green. God, he is handsome. And he smells so good.

Fred gives her shoulder a gentle nudge. "I think I lost you for a minute."

"Sorry. I was just thinking about my grandpa." *Liar!* She puts a very needed step or two between them, "You seem to know a lot about wood and stonework, Fred."

"I've swung a hammer or two," he admits. "Actually, I put myself through college doing construction work."

Fred swinging a hammer, his bare chest beaded with sweat, a tool belt slung low. OMG, am I having a construction fantasy? She feels her face redden—it deepens under his stare.

"Thinking of grandpa, again?" he chuckles.

Her palm finds its way to her blushing cheek, "Anyway, most of the living room is original. Annie's mini master is there in the front, and mine is back here." After admiring her master suite and home office, Fred heads to the bathroom, and she to the kitchen. Once again, Annie materializes from thin air scaring the ever-loving crap out of her mother. "Stop doing that," she hisses.

Annie totally ignores her plea and gets to the reason why she's in the kitchen. "So, how was your faux date?" she asks rather bemusedly.

"Interesting."

"And Steve. What's he like?"

"He's really nice and totally into Maura."

"It's the boobs," Annie chuckles.

Kitt chuckles.

"By the way, you never said what Steve is like," Annie continues.

"He's really handsome, like Chris Hogan handsome."

"Mom, must you always describe men as their NFL doppelgangers?"

"Yes. It's efficient."

"For people who know football," Annie counters.

"Well, you know football, Annie."

She shrugs. "So, tell me about your faux date."

"Well, he's a detective named Fred Serpico, and he looks like Joe Flacco of the Baltimore Ravens. But better." She raises her hand to her forehead and swoons.

Annie sighs. "Don't tell me if you don't want to, but don't make up stories."

Fred choses the perfect time to clear his throat.

Annie swings around, the motion sending her face first into Fred's very broad chest. Kitt isn't sure whether it's fright or sight that renders Annie speechless, but she scurries off without uttering a single word. The daters share a small laugh at Annie's expense, but inside, Kitt is laughing her ass off. They decide to forego pizza and head out to the porch.

"The place is amazing. You covered every detail beautifully." He takes one of Kitt's hands in his, "I didn't see a security system, though."

"That's because I don't have one."

Fred stiffens. "You really should. You're pretty far off the beaten path." He grabs his pizza, leans low, and plants a very nice kiss on her lips. He whispers in her ear, "Get a security system, Kittridge."

Screech! "Wait, what? You know my first name?"

"Checked you out, Kittridge Anne Mahoney. Can't be too careful these days, there are a lot of crazies out there." He winks, "And for the record, you look like Evangeline Lilly. But better."

And with that, Detective Fred Serpico and his Neapolitan crust Prosciutto and Fig pizza fade into the night.

THE STALKER

"Who-the-fuck-is-**that**?" He keeps his night visions trained on the guy who kissed her. The increasingly agitated man forces himself to stay tight in the tree line until the bastard gets into his truck, and leaves. "Is she dating him? What-the-fuck. I'm here every damn night—how did I miss a boyfriend?"

He turns his attention to the light that just came on in her bedroom. His anger flares at the missed opportunity to get inside the bungalow. "If you'd been alone tonight, like you are every other fucking night, you'd be asleep, and I'd be in your bedroom—watching. I had plans for you, Kitt Mahoney, but you ruined them. Don't fucking worry, it's just a matter of time before I ruin you."

Nothing faux about him.

"John, I'm thinking about installing a security system," Kitt says over morning coffee on a very fogged in porch.

"*Really?*"

"What? You don't think a security system is a good idea?"

"It's a *very* good idea."

"Then what's with the tone?" she challenges.

He gives his head a little shake, pulls and exhales a deep breath. "Kitt, I suggested you put a security system in during the renovations."

"You did? Why didn't I do it?"

Another shake of his head and deep pull of air. "First, we both know why you didn't do it—you suck at using anything with buttons and sequences."

"Yes. But you're great with them. You could have taught me."

"Not likely." He takes a quick look her way, folds the newspaper he's trying to read, and wades in. "When I suggested the security system you said, and this is a quote, 'there isn't one more thing being done to this house! I can't wait for the last hammer swinging, spit spewing, ass crack showing caveman to leave.'"

She harrumphs at the vague recollection.

"And then you cancelled delivery on the security system I bought for you." He stares at her, really stares at her, "You don't remember do you? God, you were a mess back then, but seriously, Kitt."

They sip their coffee in silence for a few. Sadly, silence is too easily broken. "Aside from the sensible reasons, why do you suddenly want a security system?" he asks.

Like magic, black magic, Annie materializes. "Her date suggested it," she intrudes.

"You mean her faux date." John corrects.

To which the Mouth of Darkness responds, "Nothing faux about him," adding a fanning hand for dramatic effect.

Kitt shoots a look. Annie ignores it.

Turning toward the tattler, John encourages. "Do tell."

"He's *hot*. Joe Flacco hot. But better. Mom's words, but for the record, I fully concur," again with the fanning hand. John's daughter just loves this.

"You met him?" the inquisitor's incredulity more than obvious.

"Sort of bumped into him last night coming out of Mom's bedroom," Annie eagerly informs.

John shoots Kitt a quizzical look.

"He was coming out of my bathroom," she sets the record straight.

"Still, you brought him home? That isn't like you." The tone is back, and Kitt is finding she doesn't like the tone.

"She brought him home, *and* she kissed him," Annie ratfinks.

"That's quite enough," Kitt scolds. "And why were you spying on me?"

"I wasn't spying on you. I was spying on Serpico."

"Serpico," John scoffs. "You already gave him a nickname?" John queries.

"Do you want to take this one, Mom?" Annie smirks.

I hate it when she smirks. "It's his name," Kitt answers sheepishly.

"For real? A detective named, Serpico? What's his first name, Frank?" he scoffs.

"Fred."

Pausing. Thinking. Pushing. "Let me see if I've got this straight. Your faux date turned into a real date. His name is Serpico, and he looks like Joe Flacco of the Baltimore Ravens..."

"But better," Annie chimes in.

"Right. But better." John continues. "He brought you home. May or may not have spent time in your bedroom. Met our daughter. And kissed you, goodnight."

"Are you finished?" Kitt asks sarcastically.

"I don't know, Kitt. Am I?" he asks sarcastically.

Before disappearing into the morning mist, Annie takes her parting shot, "And he calls her Kittridge."

"No way! No one calls her Kittridge. I tried it once, and didn't pronounce my words right for a week," John calls out after **his** daughter. He looks Kitt square in the eye, "Right?"

She shrugs.

The stunned man leaves a few minutes later, his repeated muttering of "Kittridge" breaking the early morning still and leaving something awfully close to jealousy in his wake.

Netti

John heads directly to the barn when he gets back to his place. He sits at a computer terminal and let's his fingers fly over the keyboard. "Fred Serpico. I've heard your name before—from where?" Within seconds the computer expert has everything there is to know about Fred Serpico on his screen. He starts reading. "Date of birth: don't care, place of birth: don't care, parents: don't care, married/divorced: Veronica Shields. Shit. Fred Serpico was married to Roni Shields. Shit." John spends the next several hours digging deep on Serpico and Shields, then meets up with Kitt and the girls at his mother's party.

THE STALKER

He turns the key and enters the bungalow ready to set some eyes and ears. He quickly installs video cameras in the kitchen and living room, then in the mini and master suites. He prepped the place during previous visits, so the installation is a snap. While in the mini, he rummages through books and notebooks, slipping a few sheets of paper into his pocket. He heads back to the kitchen and checks the wall calendar for upcoming family events. It helps knowing when all of them will be gone from the bungalow.

"Nana Maxwell's birthday, today. Homecoming Dinner Dance, September 8th."

He returns to the master bedroom; takes his time moving through. He opens drawers, and runs his fingers along silky things folded neatly inside. He lifts a fuzzy sweater from within, and holds it to his nose. He pulls in the lingering sweet scent of her, tucks the pink garment back where it belongs, and moves on. He runs his hand along the bed as he makes his way to a bank of windows that face *his* ocean. He is eager to enact his plan against the woman who lives here, but he likes the waiting and the watching. It's his form of foreplay. And like most red-blooded men, he responds to foreplay. Sort of. Just being in her room, thinking of what's going to happen there causes a stirring down below. He loves it. Strokes it.

Before leaving the bungalow, he tosses flowers he ripped from her window box onto the kitchen floor, grinds them beneath his boot, and kicks them aside. They land under a decorative chair by the back door, somewhat out of view. He takes a final minute on the porch sofa listening to gentle waves roll in. He is enjoying the moment, until his eyes scan the full of the back porch. His erection shrinks and fades fully away when he sees **it**, the driftwood sign hanging on the wall by the back door: **Bullet Bungalow**. "Fucking bitch," he snarls as he leaves the porch and steps into the tree line that abuts the driveway.

And not in the good way.

The Mahoney-Maxwell clan return from Nana Maxwell's birthday gathering shortly before 11 PM. Fred's truck is parked on the driveway. Kitt shoots Annie a pleading look. She ignores it.

"Ooooo, this ought to be good," the troublemaker purrs.

"Kitt, whose truck is this?" John asks.

Annie purrs again, "Yeah Mom, whose truck is this?"

"That's my truck," Fred says as he rounds the back of the house.

Annie jumps and scurries behind John's back. She peeks out from around her father and pleads in Fred's direction, "Will you stop doing that?"

"I love karma," Kitt mumbles.

After a brief introduction, John and the girls head inside. Fred and Kitt hang back. "This is an unexpected surprise," she says as he pulls her hip to hip. "Ooooo, that's an unexpected surprise, too," she teases.

Fred's smile is devilishly delicious, "That's just a bonus."

"Did you say boner…"

"I said bonus," he tightens his hold on her ass. "I really came by to drop off a list of security systems, and to give you this." He pulls her close and delivers a toe-curling kiss.

When she catches her breath she whispers, "I hope you'll come by again, and again, and again."

They make their way to the back porch where John has made himself comfortable. The men in Kitt's life get right on like guy friends, not the kind who've been through a war together, but the kind that don't need to piss out territory, or grunt, or tackle something big. It suddenly dawns on Kitt that John doesn't have friends, none that she knows of anyway. He has his daughters, he has her, he has his software design company, and he has his Netti spread. Those are the things that fill John's time. Right now, he plans on filling his time with Fred and Kitt. The impromptu get together could be awkward—it isn't. Kitt figures that the time is relaxed because both men are comfortable in their skin. Of course, it helps that their skins resemble Joe Flacco and Aaron Rodgers. It certainly helps Kitt.

Shortly before midnight, the maybe-couple walk to his truck. He pulls her tight. "John's a good guy. He didn't seem to mind that I stopped by unannounced," Fred whispers between nibbles along her neck. "How about you, Kittridge?"

"Hmmmm. Me. Mind. What?"

"That I stopped by."

"Hmmmm, don't stop. This feels soooo good."

Fred laughs deep then stops on a dime. She feels him stiffen—and not in the good way. The cop growls into her ear, "Get in the house."

"What?"

"Go. Now." The cop demands. He is gone from sight before Kitt makes it through the bungalow's front door.

John checks in with the teens upstairs, tours the first floor checking rooms, then steps onto the back porch to wait. Kitt is in the living room, a bit on edge, and Annie is riding her mother's last nerve. "Is this really necessary? The detective heard something in the woods. Hello, things live in the woods. What's he going to detect in the dark? Animals, birds, bugs?"

When Fred enters through the front door, he scares the crap out of Annie. Again.

"Would you stop doing that!" she stomps her foot and demands.

"I really love karma," Kitt chuckles.

Fred is in total cop mode when he starts talking. "Someone was in the tree line. He had a jump on me when I started chasing him. He never came onto the road, but I think I heard him when he hit pavement."

"If he stayed in the trees, he would have to exit through the stone arch at the property line that leads onto Farmington. There's no opening onto Tarrington," John explains as they all meet up in the kitchen.

"So, it's nothing," Annie dismisses.

"Not nothing, Annie. Something."

"How so, Serpico?"

"Annie!" John and Kitt scold in unison.

Fred leans against the counter and locks eyes with the young woman. Calmly, he addresses her. "Who walks through the woods at night? Who runs away when a cop tells them to stop? And who does this?" Fred puts his cell phone on the counter.

They all bend and look at his phone. "Did you just take these?" Kitt asks.

Fred nods. "There's a clearing in a cluster of trees that abuts the driveway." Fred points to a picture—it's dark so he helps explain, "That's a lawn chair facing the bungalow, next to it is a cooler with a pair of night vision binoculars sitting on top."

"Someone's been watching us?" Annie nervously chokes.

Fred nods. Annie nestles into her mother's side.

John looks at the pictures, again. "What the hell?"

"Who the hell?" Fred adds.

Both men excuse themselves to make calls. When John returns, he tells Kitt his plans for the younger girls. "I'll take Callie and Tess home with me. I've got security at Netti Farmhouse; they'll be safer there. I'd like you and Annie to come too."

Kitt takes hold of John's hand. "I'd really rather stay at the bungalow. Fred offered to stay the night. If Annie wants to go to Netti, that's fine, but I think she'd be more comfortable here with me. Besides, I can't even think about handling the labyrinth security system you have there."

John practically growls his next words. "It's time to get a security system, Kitt. I never should have let you talk me out of it when you did the renovations."

Fred points to the brochures he brought.

John nods and points to them, "Pick one, Kitt," then he kisses her goodbye. John Maxwell never kisses Kitt Mahoney goodbye, well except for the other night when he didn't kiss her hello, so he kind of owed her a kiss goodbye but—Kitt suddenly remembers that Fred is in the room. She feels as though she needs to explain.

"Must be the stress," she says as John leaves.

"Uh huh," Fred grunts.

Detective Serpico camps out on the couch in the living room—Annie and Kitt share the California king in the master suite—all of them get comfortable—none of them get sleep.

THE STALKER

He heard the man identify himself as a cop. "She's dating a cop. A fucking cop! The son-of-a-bitch has my stuff. It'll be processed for prints. They'll find prints—not mine, though." A mile up from the stone arch, he cut across Farmington Road and into a thick grove of trees. He thought about stopping on Westin to grab his car, thought better of it. He ran full out, and didn't slow down until he reached the clearing. He jumped into his truck, his heart racing—his mind spinning.

"I'm safe—for now. But I need to go back for the Nissan." He pulls a pair of latex gloves from his hands, runs his palms along his jeans, then pounds his fists on his thighs. "It's supposed to end at the bungalow. Now that the cop knows she's got a stalker, he'll be around all the time. And if he's not around, the bastard father will be with her. I might not be able to get back into the bungalow. Fuck. I might have to find another place."

The spinning in his head picks up speed. He needs to slow the swirl. He starts counting, "One. Two. Three." He starts again, this time he adds plans, "One. Get my Nissan out of her neighborhood and stashed here. Two. Get the cop away from her. Three. Fucking ruin her. Four. Get what's owed me."

Several hours in his truck making plans sets him right. He runs back to his Nissan, and on his way out of her neighborhood he drives down Tarrington past her bungalow. "I'll be seeing you soon, Kitt," his maniacal laugh echoing into the night.

He. Means. Business.

Kitt gets up before dawn expecting to find Fred asleep on the couch. Instead he's in the kitchen putting on coffee. *He looks good in my kitchen.* "Did I hear you leave last night?" she yawns.

"I met Steve at the clearing." He rubs his hand across his scruffy face.

"What time did you get back?"

"A little after two."

"Did you get what you need?"

"Won't know until we process it."

After Round 1 of their, *I'm too tired to talk – talk*, he hands her a mug of coffee, and heads toward the seat opposite her. "The evidence will be processed for finger…" He stops mid-word, and walks toward a chair that's by the back door. "Hey, Kittridge, hand me my phone."

She does as he asks, although she's perplexed about what he's doing. "Fred. Why are you taking pictures of flowers on the kitchen floor?"

"Look at this floor. It's spotless except for the flowers," he answers as though his words should clear things up.

"Soooo?" she sort of challenges.

"Kittridge, the flowers don't belong on the floor. Since they don't belong, I have questions."

"Such as?"

"Why are they here? Where did they come from? Why are they crushed?"

Blame it on her fatigue, but she thinks Fred's questions are ridiculous. She thinks she rolls her eyes before responding—she totally rolls her eyes. "The flowers are on the floor because someone dropped them. They came from my window boxes on the side of the house. They're crushed because someone stepped on them." She holds back her, duh.

Fred doesn't roll his eyes; he stares her down. "Who dropped them? Who pulled them from the window boxes? The boxes on the side of the bungalow near the tree line, where a stalker has been hanging out, I might add. Who crushed them?"

His simple questions raise the hair on the back of her neck. "Fred." She waits until he looks at her. "Was someone in my house?"

He doesn't say yes, he doesn't say no, he simply says, "You're getting a security system. Today, Kittridge." Fred puts his hands on her waist and lifts her onto the counter, the one that's generally used as a place to line up her Moscato bottles. She decides she likes this use of counter-space much better. He sweeps her hair back from her face and locks onto her acorn-brown eyes. He moves in for a kiss and stops, "Is there anything between you and John?"

"No."

"And the kiss last night?"

She shrugs, "I haven't a clue, but I do know that you're the first guy I've brought home after a date, even though it was only a faux, faux, date. So maybe there's something working in his head. John's been 'my guy' since we were in the fifth grade. And by that, I mean he's my friend, the father of my girls, the one who gives me security system advice that I ignore, and the one who would have chased that guy last night."

Fred traces the lines of her cheekbones with his thumbs, inches her hips forward, presses himself against her purring place, and kisses her like he means business. He. Means. Business. When he steps away, he takes her breath with him. "Your thing with John. It's none of my business unless he kisses you like that."

"No one has ever kissed me like that."

While the installation team from Breen's Security does its thing, Fred, John, Annie, Maura, Steve, and Kitt discuss "the case" on the bungalow's back porch. Apparently, sometime between her first faux date and toe-curling kiss with Detective Fred Serpico, Kittridge Anne Mahoney became part of a police investigation. An investigative file was opened at the Mayflower-Falls Police Department, and a detective named Serpico is all over it.

"God, I wish he was all over me."

"What did you just say?" Annie asks as though she's had some sort of stroke.

Kitt feels the stare of ten eyes on her reddening face. Her heart begins thumping a nervous beat. "Um, nothing," she whispers.

Annie pushes. Annie always pushes. "You said you wanted something all over you."

Oh. My. God. I said that out loud. I think I'm having some sort of stroke.

"I heard her say she wanted this to be over," Fred offers.

My hero.

"Yup, that's what I heard," Maura seconds.

My friend.

John and Steve say nothing.

Smart men.

Fred slips his hand onto her thigh, and begins twirling little circles with his thumb. Kitt swoons. This swoon isn't a faux swoon, or a faux, faux, swoon, it's the real thing. Hours later, after several unsuccessful attempts at the security panel, Fred pulls Kitt close, "You'll get it."

"No, she won't," is sung in harmony by her traitorous friends and family. She would offer an objection to the whole lot of them, but they are right—she won't get it. A somewhat dejected Kitt accepts Fred's see-you-later kiss, and says goodbye to Maura and Steve at the driveway. She heads back inside to find John leaning against a wall, his feet crossed at the ankles, his arms folded across his chest, a smirk upon his face.

"I want to smack the smirk off his face," she mumbles, then smiles in his direction, "Is there something you need?"

"Nope. Just want you to know I'm here, in case you want to try the security panel, again."

"I'm good, thanks." It annoys the hell out of her that he knows she's less frightened by a tree-line hiding, binocular-peeping, flower-crushing stalker than she is of her new state-of-the-art security system. So lost in her thoughts, Kitt doesn't realize that she's washed the same plate for the fourth time.

John speaks from behind. "Do you want to try the security system again, or do you want to wash the color from that plate?"

"Neither."

"You need to learn how to use it, Kitt," he calls over his shoulder as he heads into the living room.

"I never learned the system at Netti," she calls after him, knowing full well that's a button she shouldn't push.

"You left Netti unsecure, today," he said as soon as he entered the farmhouse.

"I know. In my defense, John, the sequence is just too long, and difficult. Why can't you choose something simpler like 1-2-3-4?"

"That's not a security code, Kitt, that's a preschool counting lesson. You need to activate security when you leave."

She rolled her eyes, "How about you just worry about the security at Netti Barn. That's where your computers are. There's nothing at the farmhouse that's worth anything."

"You and the kids are at the farmhouse, Kitt. You need to learn how to use..."

"Got it!" **she cut him off.**

Kitt's leaving Netti "unsecure" was a constant source of tension between them. The thing is, Kitt Mahoney does not interact well with technology, and by that, it should be noted that she is incapable of mastering anything more sophisticated that an on/off button. Yet, here she is, staring at a plastic box with numbers and buttons that activate the front zone, or the back zone, or the entire zone—and the only button that makes any sense to her is the panic button—the one that's the size and color of an Heirloom tomato. She picks up the cheat sheet Fred left for her and reads it, then reads it again. She decides that she hates the cheat sheet, and tosses it and the dishtowel she's been busily twisting onto the counter. She curses the state-of-the-art security system, goes to bed in a huff, and when she finally drifts off to sleep, she dreams about Heirloom tomatoes.

THE STALKER

He sat at his monitors all day—he's still sitting there—enjoying the show. The eyes and ears he planted the day before paid off big time. The surveillance cameras in the kitchen and the living room gave him a perfect view of the security keypads that the cop numbered up dozens of times for the stupid bitch, who failed to get it dozens of times. "It doesn't matter. You won't be living there long enough for it to matter," he mocks.

The Stalker sits back and watches her toss and turn in bed. "Having trouble sleeping? Maybe you feel my eyes on you? Wait until you feel me on you, in you." He feels that stirring. He reaches down and touches himself. Shrugs at the mediocre response. "You'd better the fuck perform when I need you to," he hisses.

Not. Mom.

Annie and Fred are up and out of the house before Kitt is out of the shower. Having inherited John's technological abilities, Annie has no trouble deactivating and resetting the security system. That means that the woman who struggles with on/off buttons is left alone in the bungalow and held captive by a box on a wall. "A plot, no doubt." Determined to not set the damn thing off on Day One, Kitt reads and rereads Fred's cheat sheet and the sixty page owner's manual. She paces. She curses. She calls John. It is annoyingly easy for the Boy Genius computer whiz, to rescue her. A key to the door, a few buttons pushed, and voilà, he's in, and they're out.

"You didn't call Fred," John offers as they walk to their cars.

"No, I didn't."

"He's a detective, you know."

"Your point?"

"I'm pretty sure he detected last night that you suck at electronics," he smirks and leaves.

"I hate it when he smirks."

Littleton College

Kitt arrives at work an hour late. She's pissed that she called John for help, that she forgot her cell phone, and that she is greeted by the wretched sounds of construction. She no sooner makes it past the evil ones when she finds campus police waiting in her office. "Sergeant Cluster, what can I do for you this morning?"

The law enforcement officer, a bear of a man with skin the color of tar, takes a tentative step toward her. It is innocuous; only, it feels anything but. "There was an incident this morning in the parking lot at Eaton Hall," he says soberly.

Eaton Hall is a beautiful building named after an original benefactor of Littleton College, the same benefactor who sort of deeded the land at Laurel Falls to Kitt's great-great-grandparents. The Hall, as it is widely referred to, is one of the original campus structures. For a time, it was a dormitory at the all-girls' college. When Littleton grew in student size and stature, new dorms were built and The Hall became the administration building. When Littleton grew again as a co-ed college, The Hall was converted into classroom space for the Criminal Justice, Pre-Law and Political Science departments. As a pre-law student, Annie spends nearly all of her time at Eaton Hall.

Kitt catches Jane out of the corner of her eye, and knows immediately that the incident in the parking lot involves Annie. "Where is she, Sergeant?" she asks in that horror flick tone she used the other night.

"Heading to Mayflower-Falls Regional."

"By ambulance?" she croaks.

"Yes."

"I have to go. Jane, call John and tell him to meet me at the hospital." As though gripped by an out of body experience, she barely registers the sergeant's hand on her elbow.

"I'll take you. You're in no condition to drive."

Mayflower-Falls Regional Medical Center
When they arrive at the hospital, Annie is still being examined in the ER, and Detectives Serpico and Phelps are already waiting in a secluded nook just beyond triage. Kitt walks into Fred's embrace, and when John arrives, she leaves one man's arms to fall into another's. John kisses her temple. "What happened?"

Sergeant Cluster looks to Fred and Steve as though needing approval. They nod, and the sergeant begins. "Campus Police was notified at 0730 hours that a female student was found unconscious in the Eaton Hall parking lot. When campus security arrived, we found an orange Jeep Wrangler parked along the outer edge of the lot. The driver's side door was open, and belongings were strewn about. We observed a female student on the ground at the front of the Jeep nearer to the tree line. She was being attended to by other students."

"Was there a sexual assault?" John asks.

If Fred hadn't moved behind Kitt, she surely would have fallen. She leans against him for dear life.

"She was beaten pretty badly, and her clothing was torn in several places, but it doesn't appear so," Cluster answers.

"Excuse me, Kitt."

The group turns in unison, as though they are on some amusement park ride in Hell. They find Maura standing close by. "Annie is asking for you."

Kitt doesn't move. Kitt can't move.

Maura steps toward her and reaches out her hand, "Come on, Kitt." She wraps her arm around her friend's shoulder, "Annie will be going up for a scan, but she's asking for you. She's been through a lot, and is banged up bad, Kitt. You aren't going to like what you see. Annie needs you to keep it together. Can you do that?"

Annie's mom nods and whispers, "I can do that, Nurse Putnam."

Maura squeezes her shoulder and tucks her into her supportive embrace. John sprints up to them just outside a set of sliding glass doors. He takes hold of Kitt's hand. "Tell Annie I'm here," his aqua blues wetting.

She nods and gives a gentle squeeze of his hand.

Annie doesn't say anything when her mother enters the exam room. She holds her stare for a moment, then silently drifts off. Kitt's beautiful daughter, the one with waist-length, honey-blonde hair, and gold-flecked, acorn-brown eyes is battered and bruised. Her bangs are swept aside, the tips are stiff with blood, and there is a bandage covering a raised lump on her forehead that is split open on one end. Her forearm is resting on a pillow, and her wrist is twisted and swollen. Kitt sits as close to her girl as she can and takes hold of Annie's good hand—a hand she hasn't held since Annie was in the fourth grade—a particularly difficult grade for Kitt.

"Mom, you can walk me to the gate, but no coming into the school yard, and do not, DO NOT, hold my hand, ever again."

Somewhat of a smarty-pants, Annie went from third grade directly to fifth grade. That's when she let go of her mother's hand, and grabbed onto independence with both fists. Now, for awful reasons, Kitt is once again holding onto Annie's hand. She presses it against her cheek and places tender kisses on each finger. She marvels that it holds the story of Annie. It is no longer the hand of a child. It is a woman's hand. "Strong yet diminutive, just like Annie."

Each time her daughter opens her eyes, she stares at her mother. Really stares at her.

Kitt doesn't know what to make of it. She just sits silently, holding tight to Annie's hand.

"It might have something to do with her head injury," Maura says softly.

"It feels as though it's something more. Did she say anything to you?"

"Just incoherent mumbles, really. Except she repeated two words over and over."

"What two words?"

Her BFF squeezes her shoulder tight and whispers, "Not. Mom."

Shedding tears.

Annie is admitted for observation and pain management. She has a concussion, a bump nearing the size of an ostrich egg on her forehead, multiple cuts and bruises, an ugly swollen-shut black eye, and has undergone a reduction procedure for a fractured wrist. John and Kitt sit by her bed, switching sides from time to time, waiting for her to wake. When she does, she desperately searches for her mother, says nothing, and drifts off to sleep, again.

A nurse ushers Kitt and John out of Annie's room well past visiting hours. "Your daughter has been sedated, and should sleep through the night. You should try to rest, too."

Annie's parents hold hands as they walk the *nearly* abandoned hospital corridors. They are too tired to speak—too wired not to. When the cool, clean, blast of fresh air finds them, it fills them. The edgy energy that dictated their thoughts and actions, all day and all night, subsides. John leads Kitt to a bench in a little garden area. "Do you have any idea what this is all about?" he asks.

"No."

"Is there some guy?"

"No."

"That you didn't tell me about?"

"No."

"Kitt, you can tell me anything. We don't keep secrets. Right?"

"John. There isn't anyone. Well, there wasn't anyone before…"

"Fred?"

She nods.

"He's…"

She nods. "It's new. And my life is sort of chaotic. He might not want all the drama."

John smirks. "I've seen the way he looks at you, Kitt. He's all-in."

There is a tone in his words. Kitt picks up on the tone. John ignores the tone.

"Will Annie be okay?" the mother asks.

"She's strong," the father answers.

"But…"

John squeezes Kitt's hand, "She was roughed up, but she wasn't…"

"He could have…"

"He didn't."

They sit for a few minutes silently sharing one another's thoughts, then head to John's SUV. They hold hands the whole ride home.

Room 412

Annie wakes with a start. Her eyes dart around the room, "Mom. Dad." She presses the call button. Twice. A man appears in the doorway. She tenses.

"I'm a nurse," he says. "I'll send someone else in."

She starts to cry. Annie never cries.

A woman appears in the doorway, "Annie," she says as she approaches. "Can I do something for you?" she asks as she takes hold of Annie's hand, and checks the bedside monitor. "Did you have a dream? Did something upset you?"

"Someone was here."

The nurse smiles, "Your parents just left."

"No. Someone else."

"I didn't see anyone in the halls, Annie. And it's way past visiting hours. You've had a very difficult day. Maybe…"

"No. Someone was here." Annie starts to cry. Annie never cries.

Bullet Bungalow

Kitt is surprised to see Fred's truck on the driveway. She is saddened to see the girls asleep in Annie's bed. "Callie and Tess," she whispers, "I forgot all about them." She hangs her head and swallows tears of exhaustion and shame.

John takes her into his arms, kisses her temple, and takes hold of her hand. He gently squeezes, "Partners, Kitt." The parental team has said those words to each other countless times over the years. Never at a time as significant as on this night. The father gives the mother's hand another quick squeeze then heads to the kitchen.

Fred crosses the room and opens his arms. She collapses into his embrace and surrenders to the tears she's held at bay. "The girls…I forgot the girls."

"Shhhhh, Kittridge, it's all good. You were with Annie. That's where you needed to be. John got the girls from school, brought them here, and explained a bit about what's going on. He and the girls agreed to let me hang out with them while he headed back to the hospital. We had pizza and played Beatles trivia for a bit. They wiped the floor with me, by the way."

Kitt laughs, then cries.

"They asked if they could do their homework in Annie's room. I didn't think she'd mind. I think they crashed about an hour ago." Fred inches Kitt from his embrace, "How's Annie?"

"She was sleeping when we left. She really didn't wake much after the surgical procedure on her wrist, but…"

Fred brushes her tears away, "but…"

"When she wakes up, she searches for me. If I'm not in her line of vision, she starts to panic. Then when she finds me, she stares at me—almost through me. She doesn't say a word, hasn't said a word, she just stares. It's really upsetting." Kitt proves that point by breaking down.

He pulls her close.

The emotionally exhausted woman holds Fred tight and through her sobs she whispers, "Thank you."

"No thanks needed," he whispers into her hair. Fred takes Kitt's face in his hands. He tilts her head back and kisses the tears from her cheeks—one by one. He eventually finds her lips and places the sweetest kiss upon them. This kiss doesn't curl the woman's toes, it captures her heart.

THE STALKER

He burns inside. He rages to the space around him. "The cop touched her! Kissed her! He will ruin her if he gets the chance. **He won't get the chance!**"

MILF.

John and the girls spent the night at the bungalow. He camped out upstairs in one of the teens' room, Callie and Tess camped out in Annie's room, and Kitt walked the floors. She nestled into her bed several times, only to get right back out. Though exhausted, she just could not get comfortable, could not release the pulsing energy. Each time she closed her eyes, they would fly open, the hair on the back of her neck would bristle, goosebumps would cover her arms, and her spine would grip with fear. "Annie." The single word accompanied her on her many treks through the bungalow, and finally ushered her to sleep—on the couch. That's where John finds her the next morning. He taps her foot.

"We already tried that," the doppelgangers call out from the porch where they are having breakfast.

John heads to the kitchen and plugs in the percolator, "The smell of coffee will rouse her," he says on his way to the porch.

"How's Annie," they start.

"She's pretty banged up, and she had surgery on her wrist, but she was sleeping comfortably when we left."

"Is she coming home today?"

"Maybe."

"Dad…" Callie starts.

"We've heard things…" Tess continues.

"About Mom and Annie being in danger," they say.

John nods. John waits.

"The man who attacked Annie…" Callie starts.

"Will he come for Mom next…" Tess continues.

"Or us?" they ask.

Kitt answers for John, "No, he will not. Once we get Annie home, your father and I will make sure that everyone stays safe. Now finish your breakfast, and get ready for school." Kitt takes her "Mom" mug of coffee to the en suite in her master, gulps it down, steps into the shower, and has a good long cry for herself.

John takes Kitt to Littleton before taking the girls to school. As they walk her to her office they make her promise to call Campus Police for an escort when she wants to leave. "Kitt, make the call," John says as he kisses her temple. She thinks it is unnecessary, but she promises, nonetheless. She updates Jane on things, who reciprocates in kind.

"Detective Serpico talked with the staff and cleared me personally. He took the key you gave me, but after he left, I remembered that you keep an extra key in your desk drawer. You should tell the detective that there are a lot of people who had access to that key."

Kitt nods and grabs what she needs to work remotely for a few days, then she calls for a campus police escort. Sergeant Cluster shows up and walks her to her car. "We kept an eye on your car for you," he says. The officer seems put out, like it was an imposition for campus police to watch her car do absolutely nothing.

"Thank you," she pushes the word through gritted-teeth. "I was just too tired to get it last night."

He takes hold of her elbow and leads her through the parking lot. "We usually don't allow cars to be left overnight unless they're at the dorms. I could have brought it by the bungalow for you, saved your family a trip to campus this morning."

"Good to know. Wait, how do you know..."

"After yesterday, we put eyes and ears all over this place," the sergeant says before opening her door and helping her in.

"Yes, of course. That's a relief actually." She thanks the sergeant for the escort and heads to the hospital. Fred is in Annie's room when she arrives. Concern bubbles in her gut. "Fred, I don't think Annie's ready to..."

"I called him," Annie interrupts.

Fred takes hold of Kitt's hand. "You're the target, Kittridge."

His words terrify and relieve her all at the same time.

Sheryll O'Brien

Annie holds her mother in a death stare while Fred tells her story. There are very disturbing parts of Annie's story. Fred runs the pad of his thumb across Kitt's hand offering a buffering touch.

"Annie was ambushed from behind when she reached into her Jeep to gather her things. She struggled with her assailant as he carried her toward the tree line. He beat her and ripped her clothes along the way. He kept saying that if he couldn't ruin you, Kittridge, he'd ruin Annie."

On a whisper, Annie interrupts the detective. "Mom, he kept calling you 'MILF'. Do you know what that means?"

"I work on a college campus, of course I know what it means. Mother I'd Like to Fuck," she says. Thankfully, the MILF moment is broken by the ring of Fred's cell. He excuses himself and leaves the room.

When the door shuts behind Detective Fred Serpico, Annie says, "He's the best faux date you've ever had."

Mother and daughter start laughing. Annie winces in pain, but she keeps laughing. It is a sight to behold and music to Kitt's ears.

Spooked?

Fred rushes into the station eager to get started.

"Did Annie give us anything to go on?" Detective Phelps asks as he hands off a cup of coffee.

Fred sips and immediately dumps it in the trash. "Cop coffee sucks," he grouses.

Steve takes his seat, puts his feet on his desk, and his hands behind his head—his signal that Fred has his full attention. The detectives haven't worked together long, but they're both seasoned investigators, and they developed an easy rapport from the start.

Fred jumps right in with a recap of his conversation with Annie. "Okay, this is what I've got," he claps his hands together once, a habit he picked up along the way. "Annie was attacked from behind when she leaned into her Jeep to get her things. She said her attacker had her before she knew she was in danger and kept her pinned to his chest with his left arm, smacking her and ripping her clothes with his right hand. Since the perp was behind her the whole time, she never saw his face, but she saw a blue shirt sleeve in the Jeep's side view mirror when he first grabbed onto her. She thinks she saw a blue pant leg and some sort of boot before her head hit the ground. And—her attacker wore gloves," Fred emphasizes.

"What kind of gloves?"

"She either can't remember, or she never saw, but she said she pulled and scratched at the hand holding her against him and she felt a covering."

"So, the guy's probably not gonna have any marks on his hands," Steve offers.

Fred shrugs. "Annie said the guy's big. At least my height and built like me, but softer. She said he was really strong and had no trouble pinning her against him when she tried to get free."

"Yeah, but Annie's a little bit of a thing, Fred. She might be off on the height, and she wouldn't be tough to hold."

"She's pretty sure on this. Annie said her feet were way off the ground. I think we're looking at someone well above 6' tall. There's something else. Annie said her attacker almost had her into the trees when he suddenly threw her to the ground and left."

"Spooked?" Steve asks.

"Maybe—" Fred's response hangs in the air before he adds. "The asshole made it clear that he doesn't want Annie, he wants Kittridge."

When Steve hears the rest of Annie's story, he gets up and starts pacing. A couple minutes pass before he speaks. "Okay, so we're looking for someone over 6' tall, built like you, but softer, whatever the hell that means. The perp is most likely right handed; he held Annie with his left arm and attacked her with his right hand. He wore a blue shirt, blue pants, boots, and gloves. Could be work, surgical, or golf gloves, for all we know. Whatever kind they are, they probably protected his hands from injury and kept him from leaving fingerprints," Steve paces a bit before continuing. "At first, this looked like a random sexual assault gone bad. The perp could have raped Annie in the tree line, or he could have taken her and her car. Instead, he beat her, tore her clothes, and terrified her. While he was smacking the crap out of her, he was saying that he didn't want to ruin her; he wanted to ruin her MILF. I'm not familiar with the term 'ruin'. It might be some new phrase being used for the act of rape. If it is, it fits with certain elements of this attack. As far as MILF is concerned, that's a term mostly used by younger people. I know you said Kitt knew the reference, but she learned the term because she works at a college. MILF isn't something our age group tends to say, and given that the attack happened on a college campus, we could be looking at someone in their early- to late-twenties. Further, the perp pointedly tells Annie he wants to ruin Annie's MILF—not Annie's mother. It's as though he wants to denigrate Kitt. His message feels personal, angry, hateful. After delivering his message, the perp throws Annie to the ground like trash, fracturing her wrist and giving her a concussion."

Steve paces a prolonged, circuitous route, then delivers his closing assessment. "Assuming the attacker and the stalker are the same guy, he's had Kitt and the girls under surveillance for God knows how long. He's been in Kitt's house who knows how many times. On his last visit he delivered a charming bouquet of crushed flowers. He's pissed, he's acting out, and he's escalating." Steve stops pacing and addresses Fred squarely, "Did I leave anything out?"

Fred shakes his head. "Nope. But a couple things popped into my head when you were rambling."

"Recapping," Steve corrects.

"Yeah, recapping. Anyway, how did the perp know where Annie would be? This is the second week back to school. He couldn't have been stalking her around campus learning her schedule and habits because the semester just started. When I was in college, it took me weeks to know the whole Monday, Wednesday, Friday; Tuesday, Thursday routine, and I had a copy of my schedule. I think the perp has Annie's schedule. Maybe he took it from Kitt's the day he left the crushed flowers. If that's the case, the stalker and the attacker are definitely the same guy." Fred moves to the window before continuing. It's where he goes to process. When he's done, he shares. "Now, if the perp didn't know Annie's schedule, wouldn't it make more sense that he would attack her when she came out of the bungalow? Or if he were following her by car, he could have gotten her between the bungalow and the school. She was alone when she was driving, and the bungalow is off the beaten path with long stretches of remote areas."

"I don't know, Fred. Maybe he got to the house late. Maybe the roads were too busy yesterday to grab her unseen."

"Or maybe he *wanted* the attack to happen at Littleton, or at Eaton Hall," Fred suggests.

Steve nods. "So, let's assume he's comfortable at Littleton and knows the campus really well. Maybe he has access to student schedules and got Annie's schedule that way. We might be looking for a student."

"Or an employee."

Karma sucks.

John and Kitt take Annie home from the hospital Tuesday evening. She is battered and bruised, and sporting a cotton-candy-pink cast on her wrist.

"Why pink?" John asks, breaking the silence on the drive.

Annie shrugs, "Don't know."

Kitt mentions that the egg on Annie's head is a tad bit smaller.

"At least my bangs cover it," she shrugs. "Maybe I should go all pirate and get a patch for my swollen black eye," she attempts humor. When she sees her Jeep on the driveway, she shivers in fear, tears up, and points to the driver's side door. "He ruined it." She blanches at the word choice, and shoots her mom a look.

When the assault victim gets inside the bungalow, she walks directly to Kitt's master, crawls into bed, and closes her one good eye. Later that evening, the younger girls go in to see their sister. They don't hide their horror at her appearance and shed a few tears. They ask her if she is in pain, then hesitantly ask if she was scared during the attack. The patient is very patient with them answering what she can, then sending pleading eyes, or in this case, a pleading eye, her mother's way.

"Okay girls, Annie needs her rest. Go find something to keep yourselves busy." As soon as Kitt finds out what they've been doing to "keep themselves busy" she makes a mental note to offer suggestions in the future. "I don't know about this girls," she says with trepidation. Against her advisement, Callie and Tess crack open a box of crayons that they haven't used in years, and march back into the master bedroom. Kitt follows them in and moves across the room—well out of striking range.

"We made a chart, and we're going to document the colors of your bruises as the days pass," they announce.

Annie takes it all in stride and suggests cerulean when Tess pulls cornflower blue from the box.

After two restless nights on the *I'm more for decoration than for comfort* recliner in her home office, Kitt is hunched over and folded like an accordion. She barely pulls herself upright before the two sides of Annie make an appearance.

Poodle Annie: "Mom, can you hang out with me?"

Pit bull Annie: "Isn't there someplace else you need to be?"

Yes, I need to be in my own bed.

John stops by every night with takeout. Whatever Annie wants for dinner is what they all eat—although the patient in Recovery Room 1 doesn't really eat all that much. Even though Kitt's main focus is on her daughter, she's noticed a distance or a distraction in John. "...it started when he returned from Madrid, but it's taken root and grown ever since," she whispers to Maura late one night, "when he's here with us, he really isn't here with us."

"Maybe he feels his role of protector is being usurped by Fred," Maura whispers, though she needn't. "Fred checks in every day with Annie in a professional capacity, and the two of you are clearly 'a thing' now. You haven't had a man in your life in this way, so it seems normal to me that John might be working through some things."

"You're probably right, Maura, but whatever is going on in his life, it's definitely weighing heavily."

Annie has been mostly quiet and hasn't shed a single tear in Kitt's presence, or in John's. She's spent some intense time with Fred behind closed doors, but other than that, there's been no sharing of the event or her feelings.

"Fred, is it usual for an attack victim to not talk about what happened, with her parents?"

"Annie is recovering bits and pieces from the attack, nothing helpful for the investigation, but important, nonetheless," he avoids answering Kitt's question.

She goes in for a second attempt. "I'm grateful Annie has you, Fred, but..." her eyes tear at the exclusion, "she hasn't said anything to me about what happened."

Fred brushes back Kitt's hair, a thing he often does, and pulls her into his arms, "Kittridge, you are part of the attack. Annie knows what happened to her, and she knows that her assailant has a whole lot worse planned for you."

Not helping.

On Annie's third night home, a torrent of memories flash and burn. Kitts holds her daughter close, or keeps her distance, whatever Annie needs her mother to do, her mother does. Shortly before dawn Annie calls out.

"Mom."

"Yes, Annie."

"I didn't know he was there until he had me. He snuck up so fast."

Kitt waits for Annie to continue. She never expected to hear what her daughter says next.

"Mom."

"Yes, Annie."

"I'll never sneak up on you, again."

"I hate karma."

It's Friday morning and Annie has a doctor's appointment. The little excursion will be the first time she's left the house, and the master bedroom, for that matter, since arriving home on Tuesday. Kitt heads to the shower, leaving Annie fast asleep in her bed. After an off-key rendition of *Something*, a soulful try at *Don't Let Me Down*, and a spirited shouting of *Ob-La-Di, Ob-La-Da*, she enters her bedroom expecting to find her daughter. What she finds, instead, is an empty room.

"Singing? That's all it took was my singing?" She smiles, then grasps the enormity of the occasion. Without warning or preamble, Annie gathered her belongings and took them elsewhere. A sense of relief washes over Kitt. "My girl is moving forward." A bit of melancholy settles in. "It's like fourth grade, all over again."

THE STALKER

He waits in the clearing until his targets leave. He has taken back his hideout, and no one knows. Not the stupid cop. Not the stupid bastard father. Not the stupid bitches. He's been watching from the tree line ever since the daughter came home from the hospital. Well, he's been watching the MILF sitting on the porch—the daughter hasn't joined her mother outside once since the incident at Littleton. "She's probably too scared to go out," he laughs, "all part of the plan," he laughs harder. "Well, she's out now, off to the doctor's office. Good for you, Annie. I have a little surprise in store for you when you get home. It's nothing big, really. You won't even know for sure it's from me. You'll wonder, but you won't know for sure—unless you check my spot in the stand of trees."

He steps from the clearing, goes to the back porch, and places a beautiful bouquet of flowers on the sofa. He sits next to them for a few minutes looking out at *his* ocean. "Fucking Kitt Mahoney. I need to get you the fuck off my land. If my great-great-grandfather had deeded this property back to himself, or legally claimed his bastard son before putting a bullet through his brain, this land would be in my hands now. Instead, *you* have *my* land. All I have is a letter from Alexander Eaton explaining why he didn't legally claim his son. That letter might not get me this land outright—but the stipulation in the original deed will."

As much as The Stalker loves this piece of land, he absolutely hates what she named the place. **Bullet Bungalow**. Just thinking about that name churns a rage within him. "If it hadn't been for that bullet to Alexander Eaton's head, you bitch, you wouldn't have this land or this bungalow. You should be grateful. Instead you slap a vulgar name on *my* place. When I own 22 Tarrington Way, I'm gonna rename it. Don't worry, Kitt, you'll be part of the name."

Ruined Retreat.

Find him.

There is no card with the bouquet of flowers on the porch sofa. Kitt's first instinct is that they are from the stalker. Annie's first instinct is that they are from her attacker. She grabs the bouquet and storms down to the ocean. "I hate him!" She throws the bouquet into the water, "…hate, hate, hate, him!" The bouquet doesn't go far having been thrown by her less dominant hand. The flowers taunt as they come back to shore pulled by gentle waves. The soggy mess lands at Annie's feet. She stomps on them and kicks them back into the surf. Over and over the flowers come back. Over and over she forces them to the water.

Kitt would stop Annie, but there is an energy in her daughter, one she hasn't seen in days. "She needs this. She needs to push back and take control of her life."

When the flowers finally drift away from shore Annie falls to her knees and breaks. Kitt rushes toward her, stopping short when Annie raises her hand and shouts. "Don't!"

The mother watches helplessly as her daughter purges herself of the pain, anger, and fear she's been holding tight. Kitt desperately wants to do something for her. Annie desperately needs to do something for herself.

Tires sound from the gravel driveway in concert with a primal scream that comes from the water's edge. John and the girls race to the back of the bungalow. They stop short. "Girls, stay here," he orders, then quickly scans for an attacker, or some reason why his daughter is on her knees in the ocean.

Kitt is frozen in place from the terror of Annie's outburst, shaking vigorously, tears staining her face. Annie has folded into herself and is rocking back and forth in the surf. The emotional fit that consumed her has passed, leaving a human heap at the edge of the ocean.

John runs past Kitt lightly brushing her shoulder as he moves by. He kneels next to his daughter. "Annie, I need to get you out of the water." He touches her shoulder. She angrily shrugs off his hand. "Annie, can you get up?" She shakes her head no. "Do you want me to help you?" After a bit, she nods. John ever so gently lifts his daughter into his arms and takes her inside the bungalow. The parents get their child settled then John places a pissed off call. "Detective Serpico, the stalker, or the attacker, or perhaps one and the same, paid Annie and Kitt a visit today. Find him, or I will."

Fred and Steve are at the bungalow within minutes. They join an angry John and Kitt on the back porch.

"Detectives. What the fuck is…"

Fred interrupts, "We're convinced the stalker and the attacker are the same person. We can explain why we think that, at another time. Right now, we need to figure out why he came back, today. Did he just happen by the bungalow when Kittridge and Annie were gone? Or is he watching them again?"

The men scramble off the porch and run to the tree line. They get their answer. Flowers, identical to the ones left on the porch, are strewn across the clearing in the trees—the stalker has returned.

Tonight is supposed to be the beginning of Kitt's weekend nights with Callie and Tess, but after assessing the situation, they all agree that it is better that the girls stay with John. They also agree that Annie and Kitt should not be left alone, even though they have a state-of-the-art security system—one that Kitt still has not used, by the way.

Fred heads to his place to grab a few things, then he and John talk on the porch. Kitt hears bits and pieces—Kitt hears it all.

"We're on this," Fred defends and assures.

John shakes his head and shrugs a bit, "They should stay at the farmhouse where they'd be better protected. Annie won't come without Kitt, and she won't come because of you. Think about it Serpico, and in the meantime remind Kitt about her Grandpa's gun—in case you're not around." John goes back inside, hugs Annie, and squeezes Kitt's hand. She watches Fred shut the door, and set the alarm system after they've left. The buttons take a bit of a pounding.

"Everything okay, Fred?"

He steps toward her and kisses her cheek. "Be back in a minute."

"Hmmmm, that wasn't an answer."

The bungalow's overnight guest puts his gear upstairs while the bungalow's overnight hostess sets the couch with pillows and blankets. Annie hovers between the living room and her mini master, quietly dealing with some emotional and physical distress.

"Is your wrist hurting?"

"It's throbbing—probably hurts from the doctor manipulating it."

Probably hurts from the scene on the beach, Kitt thinks, otherwise. Concern for her daughter settles deep as she shoots furtive glances her way. The young woman is pale, a little shaky on her feet, and seems—fragile—a word Kitt never thought she'd use to describe Annie Mahoney-Maxwell. "I want you to stay with me in my master tonight." Relief crosses Annie's face at the offer, and Kitt's face at the acceptance.

Couch canoodling.

Kitt heads to the living room after tucking Annie in, and mellowing out in the shower. She finds Fred sitting on the couch, doing something with his gun. Kitt is **not** a gun person, she refused to let John have them at Netti, but under the circumstances, she likes seeing Fred's gun set upon the table beside him. Given that she can't manage on/off buttons and number sequences she preemptively assures, "You don't need to give me any lectures, Detective Serpico, I have absolutely NO INTENTION of touching your gun." She leans against the doorjamb and twirls a long, wavy strand of her hair, "Well, the gun on the table that is."

The M.A.N. laughs, then pats the seat next to him, "Come closer," he growls.

She struts her way over, snuggles in close, breathes deep. "You showered." She breathes deep again. "Mmmmm, woodsy, citrusy, yummy."

He pulls her close, breathes deep. "You showered." He breathes deep again, "Mmmmm, lemons and honey."

They spend a minute snuggling, breathing, kissing.

"I brought my running gear," Fred nibbles into her ear.

"Mmmmm, running gear," she moans.

"We're going for a run."

"Now?" she snaps as she scooches away.

He laughs and pulls her back to him, "Tomorrow, Kittridge."

"Oh, right. Tomorrow." She giggles.

"We'll go for a run, then walk the place," he nibbles. "I want to see your property lines," he finds a moan-worthy spot on her neck.

"Mmmmm, my panty lines."

He chuckles. "Property lines. I want to get a feel for the place," he kisses along her neck.

"Mmmmm, feel the place."

He laughs again, "Kittridge, I don't think you're paying attention. I want to get a feel for your place, your property."

Screech! Moment gone. "Okay. But why?"

"The perp knows your land. He got away from me the last time. I don't want a repeat of that."

"You think he's coming back, again."

"Definitely."

Kitt snuggles against Fred and kisses him. "I'm glad you're here and that you're packing heat, Serpico."

Fred pulls her beneath him. "Let me show you how much heat I'm packing, Mahoney."

She muffles her squeal into his shoulder, and nestles deep beneath him. She likes the weight of him on top of her, is surprised at her response, her movements, her blatant offering. His hips press and hold her still. His want presses long and hard along her abdomen. He groans deep as he pulls from her kiss. Her want becomes wet and warm, her chest finds his then pulls away in concert with her breathing, her panting. He brushes her hair away from her face and traces the contours of it with the pads of his thumbs. "Beautiful," he moans. "Please," she whispers.

Their looks share their desire, their kisses unleash their passion, their movements hold no mysteries. She lifts his shirt and runs her hands across his broad, muscular, naked back. He reaches between them and cups her breast, finds her budded nipple. They rise and fall into each other. Their touches become urgent—purposeful—as though tonight is the night.

"You need to leave," Fred growls.

Screech! What the hell? She nods. She pants. She does not leave. She kisses. She touches. She thinks about begging. She is **not** above begging.

Fred brushes her hair away, and takes hold of her face. "Seriously, Kittridge."

She tries to move out from under him. He reads the confusion, and hurt that runs her face—he presses her tight with his hips. "Kittridge, I want you more than I want my next breath, but not like this. When we're together for the first time, it's going to be in a bed, where we can spend the night making love." He gives her one more kiss. He makes sure it's one of promises made, and of things to come.

THE STALKER

He is vacillating between rage and panic. "The cop really is stupid," he hisses. "He could screw the bitch right there, right now; instead, he turns her away." Maniacal laughter breaks through then quickly turns back to rage, "I won't turn her away. I've waited for more than a year to ruin her and take everything she has. **I'm done waiting. Tomorrow, I kill the cop.**"

The crazed man presses his hands to either side of his head. He needs to settle the chaos that's building inside. He tries to calm himself with words from long ago. He lets them take control.

"When you feel your control slipping, turn your focus to the repetitive or the rudimentary. Begin with counting. One. Two. Three. When you feel the calming affects settling in, add a plan. One. Get up. Two. Go to the kitchen. Three. Get a snack to eat. These are examples, of course. Each chaotic situation will require a unique set of plans…"

"One. I need the cop to be gone. Two. I need to ruin Kitt Mahoney. Three. I need to terrify the daughter off my land. Four. I need to wait for the land to go up for sale. Five. I need to make a claim for the land. Six. I need to **Get. My. Land.**"

Red Nissan Altima.

The almost-lovers say nothing about the couch canoodling over their morning coffee. Clarification: they say nothing verbally. There are hooded looks, from them—quite a few sighs, from her—several groans, from him.

Apparently, sexual inaction speaks louder than words.

The Porch

Maura and Steve park themselves next to the poodle-pit-bull mix on the back porch, ready to dive into large cups of Perks coffee and a dozen donuts.

"Ah, cop food," Annie teases.

"And nectar of the Gods," Steve says while holding his coffee cup high. "Don't forget the nectar."

The nurse sits next to the patient and takes hold of her casted hand. "I hope you've been moving your fingers, Annie. You really need to. Here grab hold of mine and squeeze. Now, release. Do it, again. Again," Maura encourages.

"It hurts," Annie complains.

"Suck it up, Doodles."

"Oh. My. God. I can't remember the last time you called me that," Annie squeals.

Maura rolls her eyes. "You made me stop when you hit the fourth grade."

"Ah, the dreaded year of independence as Mom calls it."

"You were brutal that entire year. Bossy. Demanding. An all-around unpleasant sod."

"I remember."

Maura nudges Annie, "By the way, when you wouldn't let me call you Doodles, I found something else to call you."

"Do I want to know?"

"Assturd."

"Nope."

Tarrington to Westin to Farmington

Fred and Kitt stretch before heading out on their morning run. It's a cool, early fall morning, and she is wearing a lightweight long-sleeved tee, sweats, and her favorite neon-yellow and black zipped track jacket. She's pulled her hair into a high ponytail, a look Fred hasn't yet seen. Her jogging partner eyes her—really eyes her. His reaction is n.o.t.i.c.e.a.b.l.e. Fred Serpico is obviously a fan of the ponytail. The m.a.n.l.y. reaction knocks her back to memories of the previous night's petting. Her breath catches, and her heart thumps a quickened beat. "Let's move," she pants.

They take a right off of the driveway heading away from the stalker's favorite hideout. Fred's long legs easily move him ahead, but once he shortens his stride, they run side by side, keeping a pace that allows for short conversation. She points to the right, "That's the end of my property, along the stone wall."

He nods, and takes a surveying look. The vegetation is sparse on this part of her land leaving an unobstructed view of the ocean. It twinkles with playful whitecaps inching toward shore.

"I love my ocean," she exhales.

It's still early on a Saturday morning, so they have full road access. Sounds of life are picking up around them, but no one is out and about. A mile or more into the run, they take a left off Tarrington Way, and a quarter mile after that they take a left onto Westin. The morning chill has faded, replaced by the warmth of a strong rising sun.

Kitt removes her jacket and ties it around her waist. The tee she's wearing is wet—in all the right places. It clings to her pink sports bra and what that number holds. Fred notices. Not long after that bit of "show and torture" Fred pulls off his tee. Sweat beads and runs down his spectacular torso and arms. Kitt notices—as do her girls! Fred notices—as do his boys! The man and woman are pulled from their *tit for tat* by some road activity. They run single file around a parked car and step in place as another car turns onto Westin. Once it passes, they cross the street to ready themselves for a left turn onto

Farmington Road. As they corner, Fred looks back at the parked car they passed. "Red Nissan Altima, guy in a black ball cap holding a cell phone to his ear," he says out loud.

"What?" she pants.

He shakes his head. "Nothing." He takes another look back.

They are nearly three miles into the run when they near Tarrington. Kitt bypasses her street, stopping about 200 yards down Farmington. She walks along a beautiful wall, her hand bumping off of intricately placed fieldstones. "This is my property line. My great-grandfather built this wall and arch. It's identical to the one on the other property line."

Fred nods, "Absolutely gorgeous." He pulls her into his arms. "The wall is nice, too."

She laughs big, her ponytail swishing back and forth with the shake of her head. Fred runs his hand the length of it and grasps it tight. He gently tugs, causing her head to tilt back. He gives her one of those Fred Serpico long-dimpled smiles, that she is beginning to like—a lot.

Pink boy-short undies.

The undergrowth is thick, and getting thicker, as they move further into the tree line. There are several well-worn paths cut through the thicket in several sections. She points to them, "Someone tramped down those paths. If it was the stalker, he knows these woods."

"The fact that he could run these woods at night proves he knows these woods."

It is dark and cool out of the sun. They stop so she can pull on her jacket. A heavy footfall, and the snap of a branch coming from behind them, sets Fred into action. He pivots toward the sound while wrapping his arm around Kitt's waist. He sort of spins and pushes, and they fall hard onto the ground with him partially on top of her. Fred looks up just as a bullet hits the tree next to them. He rolls off of her, pulls up the leg of his sweats, and grabs his gun from an ankle holster. "You okay?" the cop asks.

She nods.

He pulls himself to his feet, moves behind a tree, and puts a finger to his lips. He listens. "He's running." He tosses his cell phone to her, "Call 9-1-1. Say there's an officer involved shooting, and the shooter is heading toward Farmington and Westin. He's driving a red Nissan Altima. Stay down, Kittridge."

He leaves before she gathers her thoughts—she is having trouble gathering her thoughts. She stays on the ground and on the phone with 9-1-1, not listening to a thing the dispatcher is saying. Her attention is completely focused on the guy, who she is beginning to like—a lot. The guy who is currently chasing a shooter. "A shooter. Oh. My. God. There's a shooter!" her voice cracks. She stops breathing when she hears someone racing toward her. She tries to stand, but finds that she can't put any pressure on her left ankle. She drags herself behind the tree that's sporting a brand-new bullet wound and wrestles with what she should do. *Should I stay here? Should I try to run? I can't run! I have to stay.* Terror seizes her; it is quickly followed by a powerful sense of relief when she hears Steve call out to her. Her relief is short-lived when the sound of a gunshot cuts through the thicket.

Fred shouts to Steve as he approaches, "Head back to the bungalow! Check on Maura and Annie, then get out onto Farmington. The shooter is in a red Nissan Altima heading west—crapshoot on his direction after that. Kittridge called in the shooting, so backup should be coming." The detective walks around the wounded tree and finds Kitt lying, nearly prone, "Why are you on the ground, Kittridge?"

"Oh, I don't know. Wait, I do know. Some built-like-a-brick-shithouse cop knocked me to the ground, landed full-body on top, and left me for dead in the woods."

"Kittridge?" he smiles *that* smile.

"I've hurt my ankle."

Fred eases her to a standing position, leans her against the boo-boo tree, and bends in front of her. He pulls the bottom of her sweatpants up along the leg she is favoring, then immediately pulls the sweatpants all the way down, leaving her only in a pair of pink boy-short undies. She hears a groan escape the M.A.N. and wants to thank him for the sexual response, what she says instead is, "What the hell!" She bends forward to grab hold of her pants—he blocks her.

"You're bleeding, Kittridge. Hold still, and let me look at your leg." His touch is gentle. His hands move awfully close to her pink undies. He groans. She ups the ante by throwing in a moan, and with his face *thisclose* to her purring place she goes all-in with a purr.

He laughs, "Pay attention. Your ankle is swelling up like a balloon. It's probably a sprain, still, it's going to be painful as hell. You have a nasty gash on your thigh that might need stitches; it certainly needs cleaning." Fred takes her sweats completely off, wraps them around her leg, foot to thigh, tucking part into her undies. Then he duck-squats in front of her. "Hop on."

What the duck?

"You want me to piggyback you?" she asks incredulously.

"I want you to do lots of things to me, Kittridge. We'll start here. Seriously, we need to get back to your place. Steve should have checked on Maura and Annie by now and is out looking for the shooter. We need to get back to make sure they're alright. Hop on."

She hops on and wonders, *is it bad that I enjoy having my legs spread wide and tightly wrapped around Fred's back, considering we were shot at and I'm bleeding? Nope. Nope. Not bad—at all.*

Sirens can be heard in the distance responding to Kitt's 9-1-1 call as the detective is carrying her into the house. He sets her on a kitchen chair, and quickly explains her injuries to Maura and Annie. He dashes upstairs to grab his gear, then back down again, calling out that he needs a shower. When he enters the kitchen, the three women are silently pointing toward Kitt's master suite. No more than three minutes later, Fred is dressed, and greeting the officers who've just arrived.

"Ladies, this is Officer Monopoli. He and his partner, Officer Speil, are staying here until I get back. Monopoli will be on the back porch, Speil will be watching the perimeter. I've zone-protected the front of the house with the security system. Leave the alarm on, and stay back here.

If you need anything, ask Officer Monopoli. He's been instructed that no one is allowed in or out of the house, except me or Steve. I've already called John and told him what happened. Annie, he'd like you to call him."

Annie excuses herself and heads to Kitt's bedroom.

Fred kneels next to the disheveled, sweaty, stripped to her undies woman. Her leg is elevated and there's an ice pack draped across her swollen ankle. An emergency kit is open on the table, and Maura is deftly using alcohol wipes, gauze, a squirt bottle, and tweezers to pick and wash bits of debris from the gash on her thigh.

"Stitches?" he asks Nurse Putnam.

"Probably not, but she should do a round of antibiotics."

Fred stands behind Kitt and gently rubs her shoulders, "How are you doing, Kittridge?"

"I'm okay. Maura's got a gentle touch."

Fred bends next to her and takes hold of her hands, threading their fingers together. "Kittridge, how are you *doing*?"

She pauses. *Oh, he means how am I doing with the whole shooting thing. Does he want the truth?*

Fred answers her unasked question, "The truth, Kittridge. How are you *doing*?"

"I'm a bit freaked out," she shivers.

Fred sweeps away hair that has loosened from her ponytail and places a kiss on her forehead. "You've been through the ringer, today. Stay inside and rest your leg. Let the officers do their jobs. I'll be back soon." Fred takes Kitt's face in his hands and kisses her good, **real good**. She swoons. She shivers. She shwivers!

THE STALKER

He ran back to his car on Westin and drove away, but not before the cop saw his Nissan. "I was far enough away that the cop couldn't get the tag number, but the make, model, and color—even this stupid cop will remember those. He'll probably remember seeing the car earlier, and me, too. So, what? Just a guy with a black ball cap holding a cell phone. Not much to go on. But the car...I have to get rid of the car. Too bad. That will leave me with my truck—I don't like using my truck when I stalk her."

He drives the long way around and waits until it's safe to pull into the clearing. He's far enough back so no one can see his truck or the Nissan from Farmington, but he can see the road. A few minutes later, a black Land Rover speeds by heading toward Mayflower. Not long after, an MFPD cruiser heads toward the bungalow. The Stalker knows what he has to do. He gets out of his truck and grabs what he needs from the back.

Oh, Fiddle-Dee-Dee.

Steve is at the bungalow early Monday morning with two Perks black and whites, and two pumpkin chai teas. He hands Annie and Kitt the pumpkin pie yumminess, and gives Fred a coffee and a report, "The torched car in the trees on Farmington was a Nissan Altima."

"No surprise there."

"Any chance you remember anything else about the guy in the parked car, you know, other than the hat and phone?"

Fred smiles wide, "Not about the guy, but about the car. There was a bumper sticker on the back."

"Yeah? What did it say?"

"Littleton College."

"Of course it did," Annie scoffs.

Kitt chuckles at her daughter's quip, then sips her chai. Staying off her leg for the better part of two days really helped Kitt's ankle. It is still tender, but mostly weight-bearing now. She begins inching her slightly swollen foot into a shoe when Fred makes a suggestion—a repeated suggestion. "Why don't you give it one more day, Kittridge?"

"I really can't. I've been working remotely for days. I have a million things to do before Homecoming Weekend and I need to do them at the College. I promise I'll hobble and wobble to my office and stay put, and I won't even run the halls when the wretched sound of construction starts."

Before letting Annie and Kitt outside, Fred and Steve check the clearing and the perimeter of the bungalow, then Fred loads the walking wounded into his truck. He helps Annie squeeze into the jump seat in back, making sure not to bump her wrist, then helps Kitt scooch onto the front seat, making sure not to bump her leg or ankle. He leans close and whispers, "You smell amazing, like lemons and honey, and that black dress makes me want to do things. Are you sure we can't go back into the house and…"

"Hey, Serpico, we leaving anytime, soon?" Annie calls out from her perch in the back.

Buzzkill.

The college coed and the college employee haven't been on campus in days, and both are a bit tense. The pre-law student is wound particularly tight and stammers on and on. "I've missed a lot of class time, and the good students are probably all partnered up by now, and this cast is so damn itchy, and Callie and Tess moved all of my school stuff on my desk, and they need to stay out of my room from now on."

Fred watches in the rearview mirror as Annie motor-mouths. When she stops to inhale, he jumps in. "That might be my fault, Annie. I let the girls camp out in your room the night you stayed at the hospital. They did their homework in there; maybe they unintentionally moved some of your things."

"Nope. I was in the hospital Monday night. My stuff was moved around before Monday. I remember because my class schedule was missing that morning, and I tried to print another one, but I was out of toner. I know I had a concussion and all, but I remember printing a copy of my schedule Saturday before we went to Nana Maxwell's party...sorry, I'm rambling, it's really no big deal."

After dropping Annie at Eaton Hall, Fred escorts Kitt into the Administration building. His arm is around her waist, and her shoulder is pressing against him for support. She relaxes into the moment and takes a deep, cleansing breath. *God, he smells amazing. Woodsy. Citrusy. Yummy. And, those jeans and sweater, the way he packs them. He's the whole package. Mmmmm...package.* She stiffens.

"Something wrong?" he asks.

"The wretched sounds of construction," she growls as power saws begin buzzing and nail guns begin rat-a-tat-tatting.

Fred chuckles at her physical reaction and verbal animus for all things construction. "Kittridge, are we going to have a problem if I start swinging a hammer one day?"

"Not if you swing it bare chested, and your ass crack is completely covered," she hisses.

"Seen a few too many ass cracks, have you?"

"During the renovation, and now around here," she groans

"Occupational hazard," Fred smiles.

"More like a visual assault on humanity."

The detective ushers the grousing woman around a group of workers, his hand possessively at the small of her back. They all stop what they are doing to watch her walk by. A few look a little too long for Fred's liking—way too long for hers. "Creeps," she declares.

Fred pulls her close.

She breathes him in. *Yummy.*

The M.A.N. spends a few minutes talking to Kitt's all-female staff. When he's ready to leave he sweeps her hair away from her face and kisses her. The women, who have long since stopped working, position themselves strategically throughout the office hoping to get the best view of the detective as he walks out. Kitt hears more than a few sighs as the door closes behind Fred Serpico. One of those sighs is hers.

Jane Harper, Kitt's Dixie born assistant, steps from behind a big-ass potted plant and storms her boss' office like Beauregard stormed Fort Sumter. "Good Lord, that man is sweltering. All he had to do was walk through those doors, and the whole damn office is overcome with the vapors," she drawls. "By the way, I love the whole hand at the small of your back when he walked you in. It's so Rhett Butler. He's all busy saving Scarlet one minute, then burning her to the ground like the damn Yankees burned Atlanta. I'm not even sure what the hell that means, he's got me in such a dither." Jane practically pants her last words.

"Honestly, Miss Harper, I fear there's a fiddle-dee-dee coming. I've never seen you so...hot and bothered," Kitt drawls

"Ditto," the debutante says with raised brow.

Kitt's cheeks redden and her pulse quickens as memories of Fred flash through her head like a slide show—not the kind of show you'd share with family and friends, mind you.

Click. Fred on top of her on the couch. *Click*. Fred kneeling before her in the woods. *Click*. Fred holding her legs as they straddle his back. *Click*. Fred kissing her. Kissing her. Kissing her.

"Oh, fiddle-dee-dee."

Eyes and ears.

Sergeant Cluster waves Fred toward his office, "I saw you dropping off the Mahoney's this morning."

Fred nods. "Anything more on Annie's attack?"

"Nothing. We talked to the first responding students again, but nothing."

Fred nods. "Sergeant, I'm hoping you can help me with a couple things?"

"What do you need?"

Fred tells the sergeant about the early morning run that ended in a shooting, about the red Nissan Altima parked on the side of the road, how it sped away from the shooting, and its subsequent burning.

"No shit?" the sergeant says. "Did you get a look at the guy or the car?"

"White guy, black ball cap and cell phone. Not much there, but the car…"

"This is where you tell me you got the tag numbers, right?"

"Nope. But there was a bumper sticker," Fred pauses. "A Littleton College sticker, maybe an older one."

Cluster's next question is immediate, "So, you're thinking Annie's attacker and the shooter are the same person, and he's connected to

Littleton. What do you think we're looking at, a student?"

"Or an employee," Fred adds.

"Or both," Cluster throws in. "There are lots of Littleton employees who went to school here; Kitt Mahoney is one of them. And most of the current students are putting in hours doing work study. I don't know for sure, but I'd bet that upwards of fifty percent of the people on this campus have some sort of employment status. A lot of them have access to all kinds of sensitive records: class schedules, financial records, home addresses, you name it. It's all easily accessible. It shouldn't be, but the higher ups overrule safety concerns when it comes to expedience." Cluster eyes the detective and regroups. "So, Detective what do you need?"

"I was gonna ask for a history on Littleton's employment situation, but that's been handled," he smiles wide. "So, how about you do a search on red Nissan Altima's registered as on-campus vehicles. It'd be easier getting the information through your systems, than doing a statewide DMV search."

"Will do, Detective."

With that out of the way, Fred asks Cluster about the construction being done in the Administration building—specifically whether the workers are college employees or project workers. When he hears that they are both, he adds onto Cluster's work. "Can you get me employment information on the construction crew?"

"I believe that falls into the category of Littleton's employment situation, Detective," Cluster smiles wide.

"I believe you're right, Sergeant. When you do your digging, concentrate on the project workers."

"You mean the dirtbags," Cluster scoffs.

"Yeah. The dirtbags."

MFPD

Fred sprints into the squad room holding two large Perks coffees. He hands one off to his partner, puts one on his desk, claps his hands together, and begins, "I took Kittridge and Annie to Littleton and stopped in to update Sergeant Cluster on the shooting and car fire. I mentioned the Littleton bumper sticker on the Nissan, and he quickly connected Annie's attacker and the shooter as being the same person. I asked him to do a database search of Altima's registered at Littleton. Easier to narrow the search that way than running the whole DMV. If we crap out, we'll reassess, but I don't think we'll crap out. Cluster will get a hit." He pauses to take a long pull of his black and white, claps his hands, and starts again, "When Kittridge and I were walking to her office this morning, we had to cut around a construction work crew. I had my arm around her, supporting some of her weight because of her ankle injury. When we got near the workers, I felt her pull into herself; she went really small, like she didn't want to be seen. It's as though she's afraid of the workers, not just the construction noise. She referred to the workers as creeps."

"Do you think she's marking all workers or was she having a visceral reaction to someone in particular? Any chance the workers at Littleton were part of the renovation crew at the bungalow? Maybe someone came onto her, or just creeped her out, and she's reacting on instinct?"

Fred nods, "Something or someone is creeping her out. I'm gonna talk to Kittridge about it to see if she remembers anything off about any of the bungalow workers. I asked Cluster if the crew is employed by Littleton. He said some of the workers are college employees, but jobs usually require extra hands. They bid out, and the companies who get the bids hire dirtbags to work the projects. Dirtbags was Cluster's reference, by the way. He's gonna do a search to see who's currently working the construction job."

"You done?"

Fred nods. "For now."

"You wanted a review of what we have on the prints from the clearing. We lifted three sets from the cooler and the owners are in the system—Tom Francis, Kurt Johnson, and Nick

Dawson. No prints were found on the lawn chair or binoculars." Steve starts pacing, thinking, and organizing his thoughts. "We know Annie's attacker wore gloves. I'm thinking the perp wears them when he's stalking and attacking, so the prints on the cooler probably don't belong to our guy. The three sets of prints might lead us to our perp, though. According to Probation, Francis, Johnson, and Dawson are all dirtbag construction workers. They probably crossed paths with our perp at a jobsite." Steve does a little more pacing before adding, "I'd place bets, at this point, that our guy is a dirtbag. He's smart, I'll give him that. He didn't leave his prints on the cooler, but he gave us prints to work with. There are a million ways to get someone to touch a cooler at a construction site, 'Hey, hand me a soda from my cooler, or hand me my cooler.' The damned things are ubiquitous in the field— no one is gonna think twice about a cooler being around."

"Ubiquitous?" Fred laughs.

"Yeah, Serpico. It means it's found everywhere."

"I know what it means, Phelps, just didn't know you did, is all. You done?"

Steve nods. "For now."

"Once Cluster calls, we'll know the names of any dirtbags working at Littleton. We can cross check them with the ones that worked Kittridge's renovation. If nothing hits, we'll call

Francis, Johnson, and Dawson in, see if they recognize the cooler, or have any idea who owns it. Although, since the cooler is so ubiquitous, it's a long shot."

Steve chucks Fred the finger, "Here's a long shot, Serpico."

They share the needed laugh before Fred takes Steve in a new direction. "I'm pretty sure the perp took Annie's class schedule the same night he left the crushed flowers." Fred explains that Annie printed her schedule Saturday night before going to a birthday party for John Maxwell's mother, that the schedule was missing Monday morning, and she couldn't print another one because she ran out of toner. "She was really pissed that she didn't have a copy when she went to Littleton that morning."

"So, you're thinking the perp hangs in the clearing until everyone leaves, then goes into the house to deliver crushed flowers and lift Annie's schedule?"

"Or he went in for another reason, like putting eyes and ears inside Kittridge's bungalow."

Steve nods.

Fred moves to look out a bank of windows overlooking the main streets of Mayflower. A few minutes go by before he lays out his theory, "Kittridge has a big calendar in the kitchen. It shows family events, like Nana Maxwell's birthday party, and Homecoming Weekend, that sort of thing. Basically, it shows the dates and times when everyone will be out of the bungalow. I'm thinking the perp has been in Kittridge's house numerous times. He probably checks the calendar when he goes in; it's big as life right there in the kitchen. That could explain how he knew to go into the house Saturday night when everyone was at Nana Maxwell's party, but..."

"There's a but?"

Fred nods, "The calendar doesn't have Annie's doctor's appointment on it, so how did the perp know Annie and Kittridge would be out of the house on Friday?"

"He was spying on them from the clearing," Steve offers.

"And, then what? He walks back to his car that he leaves a few streets away, drives to a florist to buy two bouquets of flowers, drives back to the neighborhood, stashes the Nissan, walks back to the bungalow, and goes to the porch to leave the flowers. All that *without* knowing how long Kittridge and Annie would be gone? Kinda risky. The girls could have left the bungalow and been back in a few minutes making it impossible for the perp to do the whole bouquet drop-off. More likely the perp **knew** about Annie's appointment, and that the girls would be gone. If that's the case, the guy pulls onto the driveway as soon as they leave and takes the bouquets around to the porch. It doesn't raise suspicions if someone drives up with flowers, but parking your car several streets away and hoofing it to the bungalow with two bouquets is suspicious." Fred turns from the windows, "and—"

"I knew there was more," Steve scoffs and shakes his head.

"How did the shooter know Kittridge and I were going for a run Saturday morning? He knew enough to be parked along our route and to bring a gun."

Steve states the obvious, "Our perp has eyes and ears in Kitt's bungalow."

And girly bits.

The ride back from Littleton that afternoon is as different as it can be from that morning's ride in. Annie is in high spirits, having been hailed as some sort of superwoman, who single-handedly took out The Littleton Letch.

"The stories going around campus are ridiculous," Annie laughs. "The Littleton Letch—who comes up with this stuff, anyway? And me in the role of some superwoman hero fending off an attacker, when all I did was land on the ground in a crumpled heap," she laughs.

"Did you correct the record?" Kitt asks the superwoman in the jump seat.

"Hell, no! The fake stories made me forget what really happened, at least for a little bit." Annie reflects a moment before continuing, "Oh, and the best thing is that the top students held a place for me in their study group. It's not like they're really doing me a favor—I am top dog in my classes after all—but it's all good."

Silent winks and nods, and happy little hand squeezes, go back and forth between the front seat passengers. Kitt repeats her daughter's words on a sigh, "It's all good." Fred teases that Annie isn't the only superwoman in the truck who conquered her fears that day. Kitt cringes when Fred tells Annie about the construction "creeps" infiltrating the hallowed halls of Littleton College.

"Fred, I swear Mom has construction-related PTSD," Annie stifles a giggle, then with noted concern in her voice asks, "Mom, seriously, how are you with all the hard hats and ass cracks being all over campus?"

Kitt groans her response.

"In all fairness to Mom, Fred, some of the construction workers at the bungalow were really creepy. Right, Mom?"

Another groan emits from the front passenger seat.

"Especially, that particular creep. You know the one I mean, right, Mom?"

Kitt shifts in her seat and looks out the side window. Fred shifts in the driver's seat and looks in the rearview mirror at Annie.

Annie pushes. "Fred, this one guy was really creepy. Whenever the other workers took breaks, this guy went off by himself down to the shore. He walked back and forth like he owned the place. Sometimes he'd take his boots and socks off like he was a kid at the beach, kicking at the waves and stuff."

"Seems strange, I'll give you that, Annie, but creepy? I'm not getting creepy from your story."

"You would," Kitt chimes in, "if you'd seen him. He did the whole walking the beach thing, but he'd creep around, too. It felt like every time

I turned a corner, he was there, lurking." Kitt's arms raise with goosebumps that stick around until they arrive at Bullet Bungalow. When the guest-of-honor and her escorts round the corner from the driveway, they find John, Callie, Tess, Maura, and Steve waiting on the porch with balloons, party horns and Chinese takeout. They hoot and holler in celebration of Annie's first day back. Fred and Kitt enjoy a minute or two of celebration before heading to the kitchen to get plates and such. Callie and Tess stay on the porch alternating between gossiping about school-happenings and singing Beatles tunes. The adults meander away.

The Shoreline

"Listen up. We think our perp put video cameras inside the bungalow, probably in the kitchen and living room; maybe in the bedrooms."

Annie shivers and blanches. She moves to her father who tucks her close. "This needs to stop, Dad," she says with angry, drilling eyes, and a 'do something about this' tone.

Steve steps next to the father and addresses the daughter, "Until we find the spy gear and decide what to do about it, dress and shower upstairs. Your mother will be told the same thing."

"Annie. You should be at Netti," John pushes.

Annie leaves John's side when Nurse Maura approaches, "You're pale and a little shaky. Why don't we go sit for a while?"

John storms away and begins pacing the water's edge. He's walked a pretty deep trench when Steve joins him. "We're on this, John."

"Maybe I should be on it, too."

Kitt is busy pulling plates and silverware together and looking out at her family and friends at the water's edge when Fred moves in tight against her back. He wraps his arms around her and kisses the shell of her ear, then whispers, "Don't react, Kittridge."

Is he for real? Don't react? He kisses my ear. I react.

"Just relax against me—pretend I'm whispering sweet nothings in your ear."

Pretend? Instead of relaxing, she stiffens. Fred begins kissing along her neck, ending with a nibble to her earlobe. *I'm reacting. Every one of my girly bits are reacting.*

"I need to tell you something, and I want to tell you while we're in the kitchen. Trust me." His hands get in on the action, to which she is not supposed to react.

Reacting! She nods and leans back against Fred who by the way is also reacting!

"Steve and I think the stalker put video cameras in the bungalow, probably here in the kitchen."

Screeching to a stop!

"I want him to see us. I want him to know we are together," Fred finishes.

Kitt shivers and whispers, "Creeps." Then shivers, again.

Viscerally reacting.

THE STALKER

He watches the spy-captured images of Kitt Mahoney and her group of losers mingle and celebrate. "What the hell are they even celebrating—that the bitch daughter went back to school? Come on. I've never had a fucking party in my whole life, and these people celebrate every stupid thing. AT! MY! FUCKING! PLACE!"

An uncontrollable rage takes hold. He lashes out at his surroundings, grabbing and tossing binders of information onto the floor of the room that he's dedicated as his research center. After a particularly ugly outburst, the floor is littered with computer printouts of deeds, and land surveys on 22 Tarrington Way, and newspaper clippings, pictures, and public records on the Eaton and Mahoney families. The mess enrages him further. "Fucking Kitt Mahoney! I'm coming for you—I'm gonna take you as hard as I can—choke the fucking life out of you—then hack you to pieces!" He grabs a dagger and stabs at the wall in his research center, "Bitches need to be cut deep!"

The Stalker knows he needs to come down from his rage, "One. Two. Three." He needs to think. "Four. Five. Six." He needs to come up with a new plan. "Seven. Eight. Nine." A better plan. "Ten." He picks up a Littleton

College Homecoming Weekend brochure. He stops counting.

Copping a feel.

Fred takes Kitt outside for a few alone minutes after dinner, "How's your ankle? Good enough to get to the beach?" She nods. He puts his arm around her lower back and tucks her close as they meander. When their feet find sand, and are touched by gentle lapping waves, he moves behind her, nestles in tight, and wraps his arms across her chest, "About the stalker..."

She stiffens and starts to pull away, "Really, Fred? You bring me out here, wrap me in your arms, and talk about—he who wants to *ruin* me."

"Yes," the cop says. "Listen. If he gets into the bungalow..."

"How's he going to get in? We have the super-de-duper security system."

"If he has eyes inside Bullet Bungalow, then he has the super-de-duper security codes," he laughs.

"Great, my would-be-killer can use my security system, but I can't."

"You're not gonna be left alone, Kittridge, but if anything happens, hit the emergency button."

"The Heirloom tomato."

Fred laughs into her ear, "Yes, Kittridge, the Heirloom tomato."

For a few minutes they listen to *her* ocean. For the next few minutes they grope like two teenagers—he kisses her neck and cops a feel under her sweatshirt—she rubs her backside against the cop's nightstick. She begins to moan, he begins to groan.

"Kittridge, when this is all over..."

"Kitt!" John calls from the porch, "the girls and I are heading out."

Screeching halt!

The cop stops copping a feel, pulls away and sprints toward the interrupter, "Hold up a minute, John, I want to talk to you." The men wait for the wobbling woman to hobble herself from the beach. She heads into the bungalow out of earshot—she is not out of earshot—she is in the kitchen.

"John, we think the porch is a safe zone. Our guy stalks the perimeter himself, so he probably didn't put eyes and ears out here. We also think the stalker and the attacker are the same guy, and that he's a dirtbag who worked on the bungalow's renovation. Annie and Kittridge said there was a worker that creeped them out. Did you ever hear about him or see him?"

"I heard about a guy that went down to the beach by himself, but that seemed weird, not creepy."

"That's what I thought at first, but when I pressed Kittridge, she said that this particular

141

worker was always creeping and lurking around her. She had a visceral reaction when she was talking about him."

"They should be at Netti."

"I told Kittridge you want her there and that it might not be a bad idea."

"She refused."

"Yes." Fred moves on, "Let me get you up to speed on the plans here. Kittridge and Annie will be bunking in the master. If the stalker has eyes inside, he knows the security codes, but my being here is a deterrent for him."

John nods, "He's going to attack Kitt elsewhere."

"My guess is Littleton. He attacked Annie there, so he's familiar with the campus. I'm gonna try to lock them down when they're there. I'm with them on the way in and the way home. Sergeant Cluster, you met him at the hospital, is pulling information on a car that might be part of this and a construction crew currently on campus. But as soon as he's done with that, I'm putting him on Annie, and I'm telling Kittridge to stay in her office."

John smirks, "Let me know when you tell Kitt. She doesn't take kindly to being told what to do, so I'd like to be there for that."

Fred laughs, "Then I'll suggest that she not leave her office."

John nods, "Anything else?"

"Yeah. When Annie said the dirtbag acted as though he owned the place, something started banging in my head. He walks the beach, goes in and out of the bungalow at will, sets up a spy station in the clearing, puts surveillance inside, and leaves flowers on the porch, **but** he attacks Annie at Littleton. He watches from here, and attacks there."

"The perp is connected to both places," John offers.

"Yeah, but I think the places are also connected, somehow, too. We're running some leads. I know we keep getting pulled toward Littleton, but my gut is saying this is about something else. When Annie was attacked, the guy kept telling her that he wants to ruin her MILF. Neither Steve, nor I, ever heard the term ruin before, but we figured it might be something young men say because the attacker also referred to Kittridge as a MILF. We initially thought ruin meant he wants to rape Kittridge, but this is starting to feel like he wants to kill her."

Kitt has been listening from the kitchen.

Kitt wishes she hadn't been.

Three steps shy of a looney bin.

Fred, Annie, and Kitt are heading out of the bungalow when he receives a call from Sergeant Cluster. "Serpico."

"Detective, you should stop by."

Fred drives Annie to Eaton Hall, then escorts Kitt to her office. He purposefully looks each construction worker in the eye sending them a non-verbal message that Kitt is his woman. Under these circumstances, actually, under any circumstances, that pleases Kitt Mahoney to no end. None of the men challenge him, each turning back to their work. She is thrilled about that too.

Campus Security
It only takes one look at Cluster for Fred to know that the hyped-up sergeant hit paydirt. "I think I'll just sit here and let you have at it, Sergeant."

Cluster paces before he starts.

"Great, another pacer," Fred shakes his head.

The bear of a man fills the space as he moves about, "The search of campus-registered Nissan Altima's pulled seven vehicles during the years 2007-2017. I did a search on the owners to see if any of them had incidents while here. Incidents usually consist of college-related stuff, underage drinking, noise violations, petty theft, although some incidents are more criminal in nature. I got three hits. Brad Cronin had an extensive record of minor violations that included theft. He left after a semester. Todd Nelson, a mean son-of-a-bitch was expelled from Littleton in 2012 for attempted sexual assault."

"Any charges filed on Nelson with MFPD?"

"No. The parents of the female student insisted that everything be kept quiet. There was enough evidence for Administration to force Nelson's hand. He was given the option of leaving the College or face charges by Littleton. Nelson's an asshole and definitely worth looking at, but…"

Cluster's pause puts Fred in motion. He leans forward, and puts his elbows onto his knees. He's leaning in to what Cluster is about to say.

"Charles E. Alden," Cluster begins. "If you're looking for an all-around creep, you can't get creepier than him. As far as I'm concerned, he's three steps shy of a looney bin—smart, cagey, **and** disconnected from reality."

Fred is handed Alden's file and reads a bit, "No drinking on campus or disorderly violations, but there are lots of annoyance complaints by faculty and students. Tell me about those."

"Alden is convinced he is related to one of the founding fathers of Littleton College. He walked the halls like he was a Rockefeller or something. Thing is, he was dirt poor and drove a beat-up Nissan for Christ's sake. Littleton knows affluence, and Charles Alden was as far from money as he was from sanity."

Fred gets up and looks out Cluster's window. It offers a very nice view of the southeast corner of the campus. He begins processing when he catches sight of Annie rushing into Eaton Hall, her bright pink cast calling attention to her. He turns back toward the sergeant, "Who'd Alden say he's related to?"

"Alexander Eaton."

"As in Eaton Hall? The place where Annie was attacked?" Fred barks.

"Yes, Detective."

Fred calls Steve and fills him in on everything and asks him to run Charles Eaton Alden through the systems. He also asks Steve to review the list of workers on the bungalow renovation to see if the name Alden, or Eaton, pops up. When Fred disconnects with Steve, Cluster continues.

"I talked with the head of Physical Plant to see if Alden is on the current construction crew, but it's a dead end."

Fred's gut tells him otherwise. "We need to dig deeper. Bring the construction crew manager to your office."

Fred extends his hand to the man who is dusting off a layer of sawdust as he walks in, "Thanks for coming in, Mr. Sanchez."

"Call me Jeff. What can I do for you, Detective?"

"First, anything we discuss needs to remain confidential," Fred waits for Jeff's nodded agreement. "Do you know a construction worker named Charles Alden?"

The crew manager nods before he even replies, "Sure. I've had Charlie on my crews before."

"Not this time?"

"He was already doing a job when I tried to get him," Jeff explains.

"When was the last time you saw Charlie?"

"Yesterday. Here at Littleton. He's stopped in a few times. Brings coffees for the guys or just comes by to check on the job. What's this all about, Detective?"

"Can't say, but I could use your help, Jeff." Fred hands the manager a piece of paper and a pen, "I need everything you know about Charlie."

The manager writes then holds out the paper to Fred. "Charlie's address, phone numbers, make and model of his truck, current job site, and his friends' names."

Fred's eyes go directly to, Tom Francis, Kurt Johnson, and Nick Dawson, the three men whose fingerprints are on the stalker's ubiquitous cooler. Before the construction crew manager leaves the meeting, Fred reminds him about keeping their talk confidential. He gives the man his contact information in the event he remembers anything else. "And, Jeff, thanks."

It isn't five minutes before Jeff Sanchez calls Fred Serpico. "The crew mentioned they saw Charlie bringing in coffees around the same time I was heading into Campus Police with Sergeant Cluster. According to the men, Charlie turned and walked out of the building, taking the coffees with him. The foreman at Charlie's current site left a message asking if I've seen him. Apparently, Charlie skipped off the job right after his visit to Littleton."

Fred calls Steve, "Alden is spooked and is in the wind."

THE STALKER

He froze when he saw Jeff Sanchez being led to Campus Police by Sergeant Cluster. He's on the move now, hustling through the parking lot. With each step, he feels a bit of his control slip away. When he finally reaches his truck, he throws himself inside. "Fuck!" He pulls a few breaths, and rubs his hands along his thighs. He pounds his fists against them in concert with his words, "Think. Think. Think. The bitch's cop is probably asking questions about construction workers. If he doesn't already have my name, he will. I can't go back to the job because Jeff and the others know where I've been working. I can't go back to my place because the cops will figure out where I live. There's only one place I can go, and I swore I'd never go back there again. Fuck. Fuck. Fuck."

What if he does?

After picking up Annie and Kitt from Littleton that afternoon, Fred drives along Route 127 past Prides Crossing and Beverly Farms, eventually ending their impromptu road trip in Manchester-by-the-Sea. He pulls into the last parking space at the Beachcomber, a fantastically well-known restaurant on the North Shore. The women head to the restroom while Fred orders fish 'n chips all around.

Their meals are almost finished when Fred begins updating them on what he learned at Littleton. "...and so, Cluster describes this Charles Alden as 'three steps shy of a looney bin' kind of creepy. He says he's 'smart, cagey and disconnected from reality'. The guy thinks he's related to the Littleton College founding father, Alexander Eaton..."

Those words get quite the reaction from Ms. Mahoney. She begins choking on a French fry. Fred makes a move to Heimlich—stops short when the victim-non-victim starts swatting his hands away. "Oh. My. God," she sputters the overly used phrase in between the gagging of a fry.

"Kittridge, what is it?"

"Remember when Annie said that the creepy worker walked the beach at Bullet Bungalow like he owns it?"

"Yeah."

"What if he does?"

They head outside and park their duffs in the dunes behind the Beachcomber. Kitt tells Fred the story about how her great-great-grandparents came to own the land at Laurel Falls. "Alexander Eaton deeded two acres of beachfront property to Patrick and Maria Mahoney as sort of a placeholder assurance for himself. He intended to reverse the deed and take the land back if he ever fell on hard times. When the stock market crashed in 1929, he killed himself before returning the land to his ownership. No legal heirs came forward, so the Mahoney's had the deed certified, and claimed the land as their own. The Mahoney heirs have held legal right to the beachfront property for decades." She ends her speech with questions she does not want answered, "What if Eaton did have a legal heir? What if Charles Alden is a descendant? What if he's coming for his land?"

"If he has proof that he's a descendant of Alexander Eaton, why not go to a lawyer and make a claim? Why all this criminal subterfuge?" The detective asks.

The law student answers. "Maybe there's some sort of stipulation preventing him from getting it legally."

"Such as?" The intrigued dune-duffers ask in unison.

Annie, the tenacious pit bull emerges before their eyes. She is practically drooling at the opportunity to investigate the legalities. "I don't know, but I'm on it! Serpico, take me home; I've got some law books to crack."

As they drive, Fred cautions them that even though Alden's place is being watched by the cops, and he can't get to his equipment, he might have remote surveillance capabilities. "He still might be able to monitor what's going on inside the bungalow, so we need to watch what we say and do." The detective conferences John and Steve in on a call and puts it on speaker. He updates them on Charles Alden's possible connection to Alexander Eaton and the property at 22 Tarrington Way. He confirms with John that he and the younger girls will stay away from the bungalow until Thursday night, and assures him that he will stay at the bungalow.

Kitt can tell John is about to say something—she cuts him off at the pass, "I am not cancelling Thursday night, John. It's the defending Super Bowl Champs' opening game and nothing, not even a homicidal maniac, will keep me from watching my team." Fred, Steve, and Annie laugh, and even over the phone line, Kitt **knows** that John is smirking. She scolds the smirk right off his face. "So, be there on time, and bring chips for the guacamole, or you'll be heading right back out to get some."

"Right, chips. That should ward off a killer," he snarls.

Steve cuts in, "Okay boys and girls, settle down. A little update from this end. A BOLO, be on the lookout, has been issued for Alden's 2010 GMC Sierra. So far it's yielded no results, and it might take a while to track him. The more we learn about Charles Eaton Alden, the more focused our search will be. We might not know where he currently is, but his picture has brought in a steady number of calls, with several people seeing him this morning at Perks getting coffees."

When Annie sees the picture of Alden, from that morning's coffee run, she comments that the Nordic-looking man could easily be her attacker. "He's tall enough and looks strong enough, and he has a layer of pudge that makes him soft." Then, Annie identifies him as the creepy guy from the renovation project at Bullet Bungalow. "Let's get this dirtbag!" Annie shouts.

Kitt smiles wide. "My pit bull is back."

As soon as they return to the bungalow, the pre-law student gets to work. She spends hours in her mini master researching information about deeds, title searches, and Last Will and Testaments. When Kitt checks on her daughter, under the guise of delivering a bowl of chips and a soda, she finds the legal-researcher crouched in the corner. Mom raises a quizzical brow. Daughter shrugs her shoulders and mouths…

"No spy zone." Just before midnight, the legal sleuth emerges from her mini and proclaims that she needs some fresh air. She heads to the porch with Fred and Kitt tight on her heels. "Serpico, I need a ride to Town Hall tomorrow afternoon," she waves her pink cast in the air, "unless you want me shifting and clutching my Jeep all over town with this."

"Nope. Don't want that," Fred agrees. "I'll take you. Just call my cell when you're ready."

"Oh, I'm more than ready," the attack dog growls.

THE STALKER

He stays in his truck for hours. No matter how hard he tries, he just can't make himself get out and go to the house. The sun has long since set, taking with it his hopes and dreams. He is so lost in thought that when a rap comes on his window, he grabs his loaded semi-automatic off the front seat, and points it at the woman standing outside.

Mabel Stuart, grandmother of Charles Alden, and granddaughter of Alexander Eaton, doesn't so much as flinch at the sight of the gun. She simply waits at her grandson's truck, and smiles wide, "Charlie".

He hangs his head, and mumbles under his breath... "Withered, old woman never had the good sense God gave out every day. That's why she never tried to prove that she's a legal heir of the only family member who ever made shit of himself." He takes a quick look at his last living relative, "To be fair to old Mabel—no Eaton or Alden—had the balls to go after what was rightfully theirs. Not even Eaton's bastard son. Good thing I've got balls plenty big—I'm gonna get what's owed me."

Charlie pushes from the truck and eyes the squalor that stands before him, "Jesus, Mabel, the damn house is fallin' down around you."

"Don't you go takin' the Lord's name in vain. He's providin' right fine for me, Charlie, and he answered my prayers, bringin' you home."

"I'm not home, old woman. Just need a place to hang my head for a few days, is all."

The motive is clear.

Fred calls Kitt while he waits outside Eaton Hall for Annie, "Hey, Kittridge."

"Hey, yourself. You sound tired."

"I hate waiting around, not for Annie, for the warrant. How's your day?"

"Busy. Homecoming is in two days," She exhales a sigh which sort of morphs into a purr. "I can't wait to see you in a tuxedo."

"Tuxedo? For real?"

"Yes, Mr. Serpico, a tuxedo."

"And you'll be wearing what, Ms. Mahoney?"

"Something backless with a thigh-high slit."

The man moans.

"And I think I'll wear my hair up."

The man groans—the cop gets all serious, "Gotta go, Annie's here. And Kittridge, don't plan on wearing the something backless with a thigh-high slit for very long."

Mayflower-Falls Town Hall
Fred escorts Annie into the Registry of Deeds office mid-afternoon. A model of efficiency, the clerk points them to the deeds and deed transfers dating back to Patrick and Maria Mahoney. Within minutes, the pre-law student

finds a noted stipulation contained in the original and subsequent deeds:

> If the property located at 22 Tarrington Way, Laurel Falls, Massachusetts, remains in the deeded hands of, Patrick and Maria Mahoney, at the time of death of Alexander Eaton, and no legal heir lays claim to such identified property within thirty days of said death, the property located at 22 Tarrington Way, Laurel Falls, Massachusetts, shall remain in the hands of Patrick and Maria Mahoney, or any of their legal heirs, as so deeded and in perpetuity.
>
> If, at such time, Patrick and Maria Mahoney or any of their legal heirs, release for sale the property located at 22 Tarrington Way, Laurel Falls, Massachusetts, then an heir of Alexander Eaton, legally designated, or in possession of documents establishing legal claim, shall be granted opportunity to inherit said property...

"You know what this means?" Annie asks, not waiting for a reply. "If Charles Alden can prove he is an heir of Alexander Eaton, and if Mom wants to sell Bullet Bungalow, Alden can come in and take it right out from under her."

"You know what else it means?" the detective asks.

Annie ponders a minute, ultimately shaking her head no.

"It means that we've established motive. Alden is trying to terrorize the Mahoney women off the land he thinks is his."

Annie flips over the deed and points to a notation on the first page. Scribbled in black magic marker are the words: **Charles Eaton Alden, legal heir of Alexander Eaton.** "It's signed and dated 2015, the year Mom was given the land at 22 Tarrington Way."

The Stalker's Lair

The warrant comes through Thursday afternoon. Detective Fred Serpico, Detective Steve Phelps, Officer Michael Monopoli and Officer Grant Speil enter 17 Crenshaw Street, Mayflower, Massachusetts, ready to work. There is plenty to keep them busy. A bank of surveillance monitoring equipment, capturing images from inside the bungalow, lines an entire wall. The cameras in the kitchen and living room are active, the ones in the mini and master bedrooms are frozen. The recording capabilities on those cameras have malfunctioned or have been disengaged. In addition to the surveillance monitors, there are several bookcases lining a wall. Each one holds labeled binders full of research material on Alexander Eaton, his descendants, and Patrick and Maria Mahoney, and their descendants, dating back generations.

The only other furniture in the room is a lone chair and end table nestled into a corner as though holding a place of reverence. Upon the end table sits a tattered Bible, the name, Sonja Frederickson, beautifully written on the inside cover. Next to the Bible sits a cheap wood frame that holds a long ago written letter, the name, Alexander Eaton, embossed across the top of the stationery. Deeply grooved folds section the letter as though it had been pressed between the pages of a book, perhaps the Bible that is nearby. The letter dated, 1 October 1929, is addressed to Sonja and signed by Alexander. Fred lifts the frame and begins reading:

My lovely Sonja,
I hope this letter finds you and our son well. I think of you both, as each day welcomes me, and again as I offer my nightly prayers to the good Lord. I humbly ask for His grace so that I may fully accept my duty to you above all others. My prolonged distance from you and our boy attests to my weakness and unanswered prayers.

Sonja, your station in this life is so harshly judged, ashamedly by me as well as by most others. Yet, it is I who should be judged and condemned. You, my lovely Sonja, far exceed me in worth of character. I believe that I will hold you in my arms again. It is what brings me peace. Until such time, I will relive the memory of the night we shared beneath the moonlight near the hall that bears my name. It keeps my heart tethered to yours and my life tethered Earthly. Herewith is my stipend to you and the boy. I will reach out again in a month's time. Until then, please know that I love you as best as this man is able.
Alexander

Fred shakes off the implications of the letter and continues his search. Across from the chair and end table are hundreds of pictures tacked to a wall. They are of Kitt and the girls frolicking, swimming, and relaxing. Many are close-up photos of Kitt and Annie in their swimsuits, even Maura, coming and going and relaxing at the shoreline. The most disturbing pictures were taken while Kitt slept in her master bedroom, and the pictures were taken from inside the master bedroom. Fred nearly loses it thinking how vulnerable his woman has been to her stalker.

"Hey, Steve take a look at these," Fred points to the bedroom photos. "Alden could have raped Kittridge on any number of occasions, and he could have raped Annie at Littleton. The list Jeff Sanchez gave me didn't include any girlfriends' names. Maybe rape is part of the ruin scenario, but maybe Alden can't do it. Maybe that's why he hasn't 'ruined' her, yet." Fred points to one picture of Kitt where Alden has sliced through it with a knife that is still sticking out of the wall. "Looks like Alden doesn't care about the rape, anymore. If he ever gets back into her bedroom, he's gonna kill Kittridge."

Stepping out of the box.

As requested, John is waiting for the detectives on the driveway. Steve heads inside, Fred hands John a piece of paper.

"Sonja Fredrickson," John reads the name, shrugs a shoulder.

"She's the mother of Alexander Eaton's illegitimate son, born in the late 1920s. I hear you're a computer genius. I need a complete family tree; names, DOBs, last known addresses, anything you can get. ASAP."

"Let me get my laptop," John starts toward his SUV.

"Wait up a minute, John. We found a wall of pictures of Kittridge and the girls, at Alden's place. They are very disturbing. As we suspected, Alden had cameras in the bungalow. They were in the kitchen and living room, and in Annie's and Kittridge's bedrooms. Both bedroom cameras were dead when we got to the stalker's lair. They're all dead now, so everyone can relax. Steve's telling the girls."

"Good to know."

Fred finishes with the real reason for the talk. "Another thing, John, I hope you can stay at the bungalow with the girls, at least until we get back—although it will be a late one."

"No problem."

"The thing is, if Alden shows, he'll be armed. There's a loaded .38 in the desk drawer in Kittridge's office. That's the best I can do."

John pulls up his pant leg revealing an ankle holster and gun. "No problem."

Fred leans back against his truck. "You're licensed to carry concealed; I hope?"

John nods.

"Why do you carry concealed?"

"In case Joy ever comes back."

"Does Kittridge know?"

John shakes his head.

"We're gonna talk about this, John. But, shit man, you just made my day," Fred slaps John on the shoulder.

The gun-toting computer analyst heads to get his laptop, "Damn it Serpico, you've already got one iconic cop's name. Are you trying to be Dirty Harry, too?"

Fred laughs big.

John doesn't laugh. He hadn't intended to tell Fred that he carries concealed. He sure as hell hadn't intended to tell Fred that he's armed in case Tess' mother comes back. "Shit," he says as he slams shut his SUV door.

Fred calls out from the back porch, "Come on Phelps, we've got a lunatic to catch."

When Fred gets back to the driveway, John says, "Check your email. I sent you the Alden family tree."

"That was fast."

BATSHIT CRAZY

Alden's been locked up with Mabel for only one night, and he wants to kill her. He knows the cops got a warrant to search his place because they killed his surveillance feed making it so he can't watch the bitch anymore. He doesn't understand why they killed the bedroom feeds, then waited a few hours before killing the kitchen and living room feeds—he writes it off as cops doing stupid shit. It doesn't matter anyway. What does matter is that the cops were in his place.

"They know everything about me. They probably figured out why I'm after Kitt Mahoney. Fucking bitch! Fucking cops! I'll never have what is rightfully mine—sure the fuck won't be sitting on the beach at 22 Tarrington Way, anytime soon. Fuck, I'll probably be dead in the next few days—well, ditto for you, bitch!

They know who I am.

They know why I'm after you.

They don't know when and where I'll get you."

The – penny – drops.

Peacefully quiet halls inside the Administration building greet Fred and Kitt early Friday morning. They are the last to arrive at a meeting being held in the Campus Police conference room. Already assembled are Steve and Maura, who have abandoned any attempt to hide their relationship, John and Annie, who have brought along their trademark smirks, and Sergeant Cluster, who's set the room with coffee and donuts. Everyone has been updated on the investigation except for the findings from late the night before.

Fred claps his hands and begins, "Charles Eaton Alden is still in the wind. We were able to track him last night to his grandmother's place, courtesy of John Maxwell's computer skills—I don't know how you got that family tree put together as fast as you did, Boy Genius and I don't want to know."

John smirks, then sips his Perks.

"Alden's only living relative is his maternal grandmother, Mabel Stuart. She's the granddaughter of Alexander Eaton, and according to Mabel, we missed 'her Charlie' by no more than an hour. He left his truck at her place and is probably responsible for a boosted Tacoma reported missing from her neighborhood. We've got officers watching

Stuart's house and Alden's apartment, but we don't think he's heading back to either. We're pretty sure we know what his plan is." The MFPD detective tosses a Littleton College Homecoming brochure onto the conference room table. It's in a protective sheath, but the marked-up sections are easily visible. "Alden's gonna make his move against Kittridge at tonight's Dinner Dance. He's returning to the scene of the crime."

"Where he attacked Annie?" Sergeant Cluster asks.

Fred shakes his head, "Nope, back to where the original crime took place. The crime against Alden's family." He hands each attendee a copy of Alexander Eaton's letter to Sonja Frederickson, and waits until everyone has time to read it. "The way Alden sees things; Alexander Eaton seduced a young Sonja Frederickson at Eaton Hall. She got pregnant and gave birth to Eaton's son, whom he refused to claim. Eaton tossed Sonja a monthly pittance so she could feed the boy and he could clear his conscience. When the stock market crashed, Eaton was reduced to the same economic status as Sonja. The son he barely supported before the crash became a child he couldn't support. Eaton's despondency made him forget about the deeded land at 22 Tarrington Way—he decided he'd rather blow his brains out than live a life of destitution with Sonja and his son."

He pauses. He sends a look Kitt's way. He continues. "That letter is dated at the beginning of October—the stock market crashed at the end of October. Eaton probably sent the monthly allotment at the beginning of each month. After his suicide, Sonja stopped receiving money, maybe months went by before she learned of Eaton's fate. Maybe she laid claim of paternity, or maybe she never did. Either way, Eaton's forgotten deed placed the land at 22 Tarrington Way in the Mahoney's hands, rather than in the hands of Eaton's rightful, but not legally, named heir. Thirty days passed without anyone establishing legal claim against Eaton, and the Mahoney's were granted legal ownership of the beachfront property, in perpetuity."

Fred pauses so that everyone gives him their full attention. "In perpetuity...unless one of the Mahoney heirs offers the property for sale."

All eyes turn toward the person currently holding the "in perpetuity" designation. The – penny – drops. Kitt exhales her words, "What better way to get me to sell my land than to terrorize me off of it?" Kitt fortifies herself, "Well, I'm not leaving, and I'm coming here tonight. If Charles Eaton Alden wants me, he can come get me."

"Kittridge, there has to be some discussion about..."

"No discussion, Fred."

John shakes his head and is about to say something.

167

"Save it John."

Fred diffuses the moment, "So, the way Steve and I see it, Charles Alden will be at Eaton Hall tonight, and he will make his move against Kittridge—who apparently is going to be in attendance."

"Alden has to know you've figured out his plan, and that he'll never get the land. So, why doesn't he just give up and run?" Cluster asks.

"Revenge—wrapped around principle—wrapped around insanity. If a living Eaton heir can't have the land, no Mahoney can have it either. And it's like you said the other day, Eaton's 'three steps shy of a looney bin'. Good work on this case, Cluster." Fred finishes to a room of nodding heads that quickly begin shaking.

ONE LAST LOOK

The fugitive needs to put space between him and Mayflower, Massachusetts—more to the point, he needs to kill time before the evening's festivities begin. A drive north into New Hampshire, is the perfect way to accomplish his goals. Standing in the finest men's clothing store in Portsmouth, his pockets full of cash he pulled from beneath his truck's driver seat, he tells the sales clerk, "I need a tuxedo. Tonight, is a very big night for me."

The man who knows his life is nearing an end checks into an oceanfront motel. He steps onto the patio and looks out at the Atlantic Ocean, *his* ocean, then heads to her shore. After walking the beach, sitting in the dunes, and watching frothy-topped waves deliver hopes, only to pull them away again, Charles Eaton Alden takes one last look, then goes inside. He grabs some supplies from a pharmacy bag, and heads to the bathroom. "Time to do my hair, as Mabel used to say before dying hers a godawful blue. No blue dye for me. I'm going for basic black—in hair and clothes."

Beautiful.

"Kittridge," Fred exhales the word when she walks from the bedroom in her evening gown. "Miss Evangeline Lilly would be jealous."

"Thank you, Fred." She casually accepts her handsome date's compliment, but inside her heart is beating triumphantly.

"Come here," he directs. The very dashing man is leaning against a kitchen counter, and pulls her against him when she gets close. "I love your hair," he says in a deep husky voice that finds its way to her purring place. He takes a wayward curl in his fingers, plays with it a second, then moves his thumb along her cheek to her earlobe, where a simple square cut diamond stud sparkles. He has locked onto her acorns, which she has shadowed dark and mascaraed heavily. "Beautiful. You are beautiful." He leans Kitt back and admires her black, floor length, halter gown, which is clinging in all the right places and announcing her girls' pleasure with his attention. His hands caress, then possess, her naked back. "Turn around," he growls, then moans.

Not only does she turn, but she walks away. She is wearing four-inch heels, and when she reaches for a bracelet off the table, she makes sure Fred catches a glimpse of an ankle strap through a slit that runs the gown from floor to thigh. She smiles at his moan. Her date is so caught in his headspace that he misses that she's moved back to him. "Fred. Earth to Fred," she chuckles. "Can you help me with my bracelet, please?"

"Do you want it on?" he stammers.

"Yes. If you don't mind," she chuckles again.

Fred nearly drops the bracelet twice before being rescued by Annie. "Give me that," she says as she hip-chucks "butterfingers" out of the way. "You shoot guns for a living, Serpico, but you can't clasp a bracelet. Maybe we should rethink this whole 'trap the bad guy plan' for tonight." Annie laughs nervously.

Fred and Kitt don't respond, they simply watch the fingers on Annie's casted hand deftly fasten her mother's bracelet.

"Let's move," the dashing man says as he ushers the stunning women to the door and sets security. Fred halts Annie on the driveway, "I won't let anything happen to your mom."

"I hope not, Serpico, because she really deserves to finish."

"Finish what?" he asks.

"Falling in love with you," Annie whispers, before planting a peck on Serpico's cheek.

WELCOME TO THE LITTLETON COLLEGE
HOMECOMING WEEKEND
DINNER DANCE

The Homecoming Dinner Dance is *the* social event of the College, each year. It is also the most significant fundraising event. Unlike monies raised through the Annual Fund or capital campaigns, the proceeds from the Dinner Dance are earmarked exclusively for the College's Endowment Fund, which is Kitt's baby. As Director of Institutional Advancement, she constantly impresses upon the Board of Trustees, administrators, faculty, staff, and donors that... "If you want a healthy college, you need a healthy endowment." This evening, Kitt and members of her team will be front and center. She will be seeking the ear of major donors, leaving her tuxedoed hunk ample time to hunt a maniac.

Eaton Hall looks stunning. Ground lights shine brightly on the blonde brick, three-story Neoclassic building with twin four-story turrets on either side. The classrooms inside each tower have been designated as alumni gathering spaces. Graduating years ending with even numbers will meet in classrooms on the second floor, and odd numbered years on the third. Across the back exterior of The Hall are two walkways at the second and third floor levels. This evening, they will be used by guests for after-dinner dancing. Fashioned with a thousand tiny lights twined through and around the black iron railings, the walkways overlook an ornamental tree-lined garden patio. Sloping away from the rows of trees is a grassy knoll that edges a lovely lily pond. Its walking bridge is similarly fashioned with hundreds of twinkling lights, rendering it positively ethereal. The grassy area will soon fill with students dressed in their finest, who will picnic and dance along the pond while the real festivities take place in Eaton Hall. The lily pond picnic-dance is a well-attended tradition—one that Kitt enjoyed immensely during her undergraduate years.

When Fred escorts his date inside, she is taken aback by the beauty of the ballroom. "It's perfect." The grandeur of the space cannot be overstated. A wall of three-story windows and twin fireplaces dominate the room, wide-plank oak floors shine underfoot, and black wrought iron chandeliers light from above. Most of the floorspace is set for dining, with white linen and lace-draped tables of eight, upon which sit highly-glossed white place settings and cut crystal stemware. Squat, square vases showcase arrangements of black-centered anemones and white roses.

Beyond the dining area and dance floor is an outdoor patio. Soft sounds of a string quartet lift on a breeze and draw the couple near. They spot Steve and Maura standing near a café table at the tree line, holding hands and peering into one another's eyes. They look like movie stars— seriously, they look like movie stars. Maura is beyond va-va-va-voom in a fire engine-red, tank top, fit and flare gown. Her makeup is flawless, and she's swept her luscious wavy red hair to one side, leaving it loose across her shoulder. She wears no jewelry—something about not gilding a lily is apt. Steve is in a tuxedo very similar to Fred's. Both men wear the hell out of them, and are simply dashing—Fred, ever so, in a James Bond kind of way. *Oh James, let me be your Octopussy,* tramps through Kitt's mind.

The Dinner Dance is open to all of Littleton College, but the ticket price is too steep for most students to attend. Perhaps that is why Annie stands out in the crowd, or more likely she stands out because she looks gorgeous. The pixie-girl is in a hot-pink, knee length, backless lace sheath, and four-inch black gladiator heels. She said she chose the dress to match her cast, and the heels to give her height. Her stick-straight, honey-colored hair hangs long down her back, and her bangs cover the injury to her forehead. Gold hoop earrings and gold stacked bangle bracelets on her non-casted wrist complete her look.

Sergeant Cluster is sitting with Annie at a bistro-style table. He is point man for Annie, Maura, and Kitt, should Alden appear. Fred and Steve need to focus on the homicidal maniac, so Cluster has been assigned as bodyguard. The big bear of a man cleans up nicely, and he and Annie are clearly having fun together.

When the group heads back inside, Fred runs the plan for the evening. "Stationed throughout the grounds are tuxedo-clad Littleton officers. Steve, Cluster, and I will be inside the ballroom most of the evening. MFPD Officers Monopoli and Speil are already stationed on the second floors of the east and west turrets. I expect Alden to make a move whenever people are in motion. Dinner will most likely be uneventful."

It is. Introductions, conversations, and speeches are made with no sign of Alden. Salads, dinners, coffees, and desserts are served with no sign of Alden. Fred leans close, alternating between telling his date that she is beautiful, and telling his stalking victim that his gut tells him this is the night. That's what he is doing when his phone rings. Jeff Sanchez's name is on Fred's caller ID.

"Jeff, what can I do for you?"

"Are you at Eaton Hall?"

"Yeah. Why?"

"Charlie's headed that way. He's in a black tuxedo. And Detective, he dyed his hair black as coal."

"Jeff, where is he right now?"

"He just entered The Hall."

Fred speaks into his mouthpiece, "Alden's on campus, just entering Eaton Hall. He's in a black tuxedo, and he's dyed his hair black."

Kitt sends Fred a *please be careful* look. He kisses the top of her hand and gives her a wink.

Flying solo.

The detectives leave the ballroom just as the dinner crowd fills the space around them in the foyer. A steady stream of partygoers moves toward the east and west turrets to get to restrooms, classrooms, and outdoor walkways off the second and third floors. Fred and Steve show their badges. "Please return to the ballroom. An announcement will be made as to when you can return to the foyer," Fred says with a touch of authority, but no outward show of concern. As soon as the guests leave, he stations two Littleton cops at the turret doors, "Don't let anyone up. Alden was seen entering Eaton Hall within the last few minutes. He's wearing a black tux and has dyed his hair black. Not much to go on, I know. Watch your back. He's armed and dangerous."

Fred and Steve split up.

Fred calls instructions into his mouthpiece, "Officer Monopoli, Detective Phelps is heading to the west turret. Meet him on floor two. Officer Speil, I'm heading to the east turret. Meet me on floor two. We'll do a search of the classrooms before they're overrun by alumni." Fred exits the stairway on the second floor at the opposite end from Officer Speil. They move in sequence, one of them entering a classroom while the other watches the corridor. Chatter from Steve over

Fred's headset confirms that the same procedure is being followed in the west turret.

Halfway down the corridor, Officer Speil exits a classroom. "There's a locked door inside. I looked in the window, and there's a set of stairs leading up," the young officer informs.

"Hey Cluster, we just found a locked door in one of the classrooms on floor two on the backside of the building. There are stairs behind the door heading up. Please advise."

Silence.

"Cluster."

Silence.

Fred grabs his cell phone.

Charles Alden approaches a group of men enjoying a cigar and snifter of brandy outside Eaton Hall. "Alexander Frederickson," he says, as he shakes the men's hands. "It seems as though I've been abandoned by my wife, Sonja. She's busy with fundraising. Mind if I join you?"

The cigar-smoking and brandy-snifting men welcome him to the fold once he agrees not to hit them up for donations.

"We're flying solo ladies. My communication equipment just cut out. Please stay together," Sergeant Cluster informs.

Kitt grabs hold of Maura's arm, "Let's find a table on the patio. My ankle is killing me."

"I bet it's the four-inch stilettos," Nurse Maura opines sarcastically.

"But the dress needed heels, sexy heels, heels that would make Fred's jaw drop."

Maura dips her head and smiles in womanly understanding, "Say no more."

They are interrupted by a voice over Kitt's shoulder, "Excuse me, Ms. Mahoney, do you have a few minutes?"

She turns to find Marcus Fletcher, a dear friend and fellow alum, at her shoulder. The suave, and impeccably dressed man is President and CFO of Fletcher Industries, and a major Littleton donor. "Of course, Marcus," she beams as he pecks her cheek and escorts her to the patio.

Cluster, Annie, and Maura are quick on Kitt's four-inch stilettoed heels.

Alden watches **her** emerge from the ballroom on the arm of a man he doesn't recognize. He scoffs, "The bitch's daughter, her slutty friend, and Sergeant Clusterfuck. They just can't leave her alone. Well, stay close, assholes, the fun's about to begin." Alden knows the place is crawling with cops, but he doesn't care. It is all going to end tonight. He will be dead before the night is over—she will be dead, too. The only question now is how many others will be dead with them?

Sheryll O'Brien

Marcus leads Kitt to a bistro table just off the edge of the patio. Her shadows file in behind, ostensibly deep in conversation. *They aren't the least bit conspicuous,* she giggles.

"How are you doing, Kitt?"

As a major donor and board member, Marcus was informed about the shooting at the bungalow. There were discussions between the Board and Administration as to whether she should attend this evening, but since it is a high-profile fundraiser and safety measures were put in place, everyone agreed that she needed to be at the event.

"I'm fine, Marcus," she says as she gives him her—see I'm not afraid of a homicidal killer—killer smile.

"Well, you look no worse for wear. In fact, you look lovely this evening," Marcus beams genuine affection.

"You clean up mighty good, yourself." She leans in and whispers, "Would you mind if I slip off my heels? They seem to be aggravating my ankle."

He nods. "Please, make yourself comfortable. If I remember correctly, you did a similar thing when our group picnicked at the lily pond on a night such as this."

"That was *ages* ago. My feet were killing me that night too, but not because of a shooting." She begins to laugh, stops abruptly. A chill runs her spine, and the memory of a bullet being fired at her in the woods pushes free. Her face drains of color, and her hands begin trembling.

Marcus leans forward, "Kitt. Kitt. Are you…"

Detective Serpico trusts that Sergeant Cluster has everything under control and isn't answering because his headset cut out. He knows that the sergeant will call if he needs him. Besides, the ground team has eyes on him and the girls, and none of them are trying to contact Fred. He needs to focus on Alden, and he needs help. He hits send on his cell. "Jeff, it's Serpico. I'm on floor two of the east turret. There's a locked door with stairs behind them."

"They lead to the fourth floor balcony, Detective."

"The balcony overlooks the patio and lawn, right?"

"Yeah, you'll be able to see everything, all the way down to the lily pond. Do you want in?"

"Yeah."

"I'm coming up," Jeff says before cutting off.

And shots ring out.

Alden excuses himself from the cigar and brandy set and heads further into the crowd. *I bet I can get a dozen shots off before anyone blinks an eye.* He steps from the tree line behind Sergeant Cluster, raises his gun, and pulls the trigger.

Cluster falls hard.

Two more shots are fired into the crowd and pandemonium breaks out. People begin running and screaming. Two fall to the ground.

Marcus and Kitt jump from their seats. He reaches across the table for her hand, "Kitt!" He has it, then loses it, as she is pulled back against Alden's chest, her feet left dangling high above the ground. She squeezes her eyes shut when she feels Alden's gun pressed tight against her head.

"Stop moving, bitch," he spits into her ear. He moves the gun away and shoots at two tuxedoed men moving through the ornamental tree line. They take cover, at the same moment that Annie charges toward her mother.

"Mom!"

"Don't!" Kitt yells.

Marcus pulls Annie back against him, struggling to keep her from rushing Alden.

Maura silently drops to Cluster's side, checking for a pulse and breathing. She moves his jacket aside, checks his wound, and applies pressure with a balled up tablecloth. She begins encouraging her patient, knowing full well he is critically wounded, "Stay with me. Come on, stay with me David."

"Cluster," Kitt chokes through bubbling fear.

"Shut the fuck up!" Alden yells.

She goes still against his chest and locks eyes with Annie as the madman edges them back through the grove of ornamental trees.

"Mom!" Annie screams, followed immediately by Marcus' plea, "Annie, don't!"

Alden raises his gun and fires at Annie and Marcus. They fall to the ground. Kitt tries to scream "Annie!" but it gets caught by her fear and anguish. Her captor turns and tosses her onto his hip, carrying her as though she is a rag doll. He is crushing her ribs so tightly against him that she can barely breathe. She supposes it doesn't matter since she is too terrified to breathe—too terrified not to. *These may be my final breaths.*

Steve and Officer Monopoli run the corridors until they reach the second floor walkway. It is empty. Steve scans the lawn for Alden; sees that Cluster is down and Maura is doing chest compressions. He yells to her—she tries to find his voice in all the confusion and noise.

"Where's Kitt!?"

She points through the trees, "He took her." She gets back to Cluster and is joined by two men who identify themselves as doctors. The three of them work to keep the sergeant alive, while the wail of ambulances taunt from a distance. "Come on, come on. Hurry, please," she begs.

Fred and Speil push through the throng of people clogging the foyer and ballroom. They burst onto the patio seconds before Steve and Monopoli.

"Alden took Kitt through the back trees," Steve yells from behind.

The detectives run toward the parking lot on the front side of Eaton Hall and throw themselves into Fred's truck. They get stuck in the mad dash of people fleeing the scene of a shooting. Monopoli and Speil begin clearing a path for the detectives and the incoming ambulance.

"Fuck. Fuck. Fuck. He's taking her to the bungalow," Fred yells as he bangs his hands against the steering wheel.

Get Grandpa's gun.

Alden fists Kitts hair and jabs his gun in her ribs, "Move!"

Her feet alternate between being dragged and being lifted off the ground. The bottoms are being ripped from the rough pavement, and there might be a shard of glass imbedded deep in her right foot. Her ankle feels as badly as it did when she first hurt it.

"Hurry the fuck up, bitch." He drags her through valet parking and pushes her into the passenger seat of a black Tacoma. "Move over," he digs his gun deeper into her ribs.

She yelps in pain.

"Shut up and drive."

Her hands shake uncontrollably and her eyes blind with tears. She's finding it hard to think through the fear that owns her. It takes her a minute to figure out that she needs to drive up onto a grassy section to get out of the parking spot. She moves the vehicle forward and in doing so she hits the truck's tail against the car on her left. She starts to cry.

"Stop crying, or I'll give you something to cry about!" he screams. "Don't do anything stupid. Just drive to my bungalow, the one you named Bullet Bungalow, you fucking bitch. Well, it's time to make the vulgar name count for something. First a bullet for you, then a bullet for me. It all ends tonight!"

Her mind starts racing.

Beach. Run to the beach. I can't run. Porch. There's nothing to use as a weapon. Bungalow. If he takes me inside, he'll have to deactivate the alarm. There will be time at the door. The kitchen door. What's in the kitchen by the alarm system? The kitchen counter. Bottles of Moscato are on the counter. Grab a bottle of Moscato. Hit the fuck out of him with the bottle. Get to the home office. Get Grandpa's gun. Get to the home office. Get Grandpa's gun. Get to the home office. Get Grandpa's gun.

Her mind jumps to a conversation she had with Fred.

"John said there's a gun in the bungalow. Where is it?" Fred asked.

"My home office. It's hidden," she said shaking her head.

"Kittridge, you need a plan. If anything happens, you need to go to headspace that's already planned for danger. If the stalker gets into the house, get to the home office, get Grandpa's gun."

She shook her head, "I don't know how to use it, Fred."

He took hold of her shoulders and squeezed. "You pick up the gun and you pull the trigger. You either save yourself, or you die. Pick up the gun, and pull the trigger."

Make a plan: hit it him with the bottle – get to the home office – get Grandpa's gun – pull the trigger. The words become her mantra.

Fred and Steve, Monopoli and Speil, finally hit the road. They are twenty minutes out and know that whatever happens at the bungalow will happen before they get there. Fred starts a mantra, "Get to the home office, get Grandpa's gun…get the gun…get the gun…get the gun."

"There's a gun?" Steve interrupts.

"Her grandfather's .38 Smith and Wesson Special. I loaded it and put it in her desk drawer."

Steve picks up Fred's mantra, "Get to the home office, get Grandpa's gun…get the gun…get the gun…get the gun."

Alden drags Kitt across the truck's seat by her hair and bangs her out the passenger side. Her feet land hard on the driveway, and her ankle buckles to the side. She manages to stay upright while he drags her across the rough gravel. He is breathing heavy, but still, she finds it, the sound of *her* ocean, there in the background of her life—the life she may be losing. Tears threaten. She pushes them back and swallows them hard. He lets go of her hair and grabs hold of her bicep. They thump up the porch stairs, and he throws her against a wall. She hits hard, banging the back of her head hard. She looks up in time to see the wood sign dislodge and fall. It lands at her feet: **Bullet Bungalow**. Her mind fills with an image of her great-great-grandmother flourishing the sign of the cross and uttering the words, "O Signore!" *She is calling out to me.* She closes her eyes and waits for the bullet that will end her life. *Sirens. Sirens sound from Farmington Road. Help is on Farmington Road.*

Alden grabs her arm again. "Get inside." He pushes her between him and the back door. He grabs a key from his pocket and unlocks the door, quickly punches in the security code. Makes a mistake. Begins again.

Somehow Kitt's mind wanders. *I forgot to tell Fred about the key in my desk at work. I never told Fred that I ...* She hangs her head at the thought of Fred Serpico.

The momentum from his opening the door separates them a fraction of an inch. The maniac grabs her hair and yanks hard. He wedges her between him and the kitchen counter while he bangs at the security code. She finds an inch between them, and pushes her ass hard against him, reaches for a bottle of Moscato, hip-chucks him several inches away, turns and swings. The bottle connects with the side of his head—not by much—but enough. He stumbles back, she pushes him hard and hobbles away as he falls backwards over a chair.

She makes it to the bedroom, and slams the door closed and locks it. She stumbles through the room and into the home office and locks that door. She is at the desk and pulling open the drawer that holds her Grandpa's gun when she hears the first shot and the bedroom door being kicked aside.

"You fucking bitch!"

She hears him storm through the room and bang himself against the home office door. *He's going to shoot out the lock!* She drops behind the desk and waits. As soon as the madman's shot rings out and she hears the sound of the door being kicked aside, she jumps up and shoots. Twice. Alden stumbles back, his shoulder hitting against the doorjamb, causing him to twist. When he falls, he lands on his side. Kitt ducks back down behind the desk and listens to a man moan himself to death.

Fuck no!

Fred heard the first shot. "No!"

Fred heard the second shot. "No! No!"

Fred heard the third and fourth shots. "Fuck, Noooo!"

He jams his truck into park before it comes to a stop, throws open the driver's door, and races to the bungalow. An eerie silence comes from inside. He enters, gun drawn, Steve is tight on his heels. Emergency sirens and lights break the stillness outside, but don't cut the eerie feel. There is no sound inside the bungalow.

Fred and Steve step over a downed kitchen chair and move to either side of the bedroom door. Fred peeks in and sees Alden down just outside the home office. He trains his weapon at the man and calls out, "Kittridge!"

Nothing.

"Kittridge!"

Nothing.

His heart drops.

"Kittridge! It's Fred," his heart lifts when he hears a mumble.

"Mississippi. Mississippi. Mississippi."

Fred steps into the bedroom. Steve steps into the bedroom. They keep their weapons on Alden. Steve goes to the stalker/attacker/fucker and feels for a pulse. He shakes his head and smiles, "She got the gun."

Fred steps over Alden, remaining outside the home office and calls out, "Kittridge. It's Fred. You need to put down the gun. Alden is dead, Kittridge. You are safe. You need to put down the gun and stand up. Come on, sweetheart. I promise, it's all over. Put down the gun and stand up."

Kitt doesn't stand up; she can't stand up. She crawls from behind the desk, and when she is in open floorspace she collapses.

"Steve, get an EMT in here!"

Seizing the day.

Kitt was on the fifty-fifth Mississippi when Alden stopped moaning. She figures that means he lived for nearly a minute after she shot him. Twice. That was the thought that tumbled through her head as the ambulance headed toward Mayflower-Falls Regional. As emergency personnel work on her, she hears one of them say, "The Littleton College cop is in surgery. It's nothing short of a miracle that Maura Putnam kept that man alive."

My daughter. Is my daughter alive? The words start banging in her head. She tries to shield her eyes from the bright light above, then tries to sit up. Her shoulders are gently pushed back.

"You're safe," she hears a woman say.

Kitt thrashes her head back and forth as the banging inside picks up speed. *No. No. No. Is Annie alive?* She pushes hard against the hands holding her down. She surrenders, but not before she hears her daughter's voice.

"Mom? Is that my mother?" Annie calls from outside her room.

A nurse from Kitt's team joins her daughter in the hall, "Your mother is being worked on. She's pretty banged up and is being evaluated for a concussion. Let's get you settled, and we will bring you to see her soon."

Fred and Steve are waiting in Kitt's holding room when she returns from a CT-scan. Once Steve sees that Kitt is this side of living, he excuses himself. He gives Fred a slap on his shoulder and says, "She got the gun."

Fred smiles as he moves toward Kitt. His smile doesn't go anywhere near reaching his eyes. "Kittridge, you had me scared, sweetheart."

She rolls her eyes, "Yeah, sorry about that," she croaks.

Fred puts his hand onto her forehead and brushes back a mess of curls. "Kittridge," his voice breaks. He leans down and presses a kiss to her lips, "I thought I lost you."

Annie knocks on the doorjamb, "Can I come in?"

Fred moves a chair next to Kitt's bed and helps Annie into it.

"Mom, I thought..." she says before completely unravelling. She sobs herself into quite a state, while holding her mother's hand in a vice grip. Within an hour of sitting by her mother's bedside, she is mumbling things from her own experience with the madman, and recounting things that happened earlier in the evening. Kitt is so grateful when Nurse Maura comes to her room.

After checking on her best friend forever she encourages Annie to go with her. "Come on,

Doodles. We'll grab a shower, and talk. Your mom is safe now. You are safe now. A shower will help. Let's go."

Despite a concussion, a reinjured ankle, torn apart and stitched together feet, three bruised ribs, and ringing in her ears from the shooting, she insists on being taken to the vigil being held outside the operating room. "I really need to be with my family and friends," she explains to the medical staff. They admit her to a room, then allow Fred to take her to Cluster, so long as he promises to make her stay in the wheelchair.

They pass countless people from Littleton College who fill waiting rooms on several floors, then find Steve, Officers Monopoli and Speil, Jeff Sanchez, Marcus Fletcher, and Jane Harper pacing the corridors outside the surgical unit. They smile as Fred and Kitt join them.

Annie and Maura step off an elevator an hour or so later. Nurse Putnam's encouraging voice cuts the silence, "Come on, Annie. You're safe. Your mother is safe." Both women have showered and changed into scrubs; the effort stripping away their last reserve of emotional strength. Maura steps away from Annie and walks to Steve. The nurse and the detective wrap their arms around one another and hold tight. "The fraternization police are watching and I don't give a damn. I love you, Steve Phelps." Maura kisses her man, welcomes his strong embrace, then lets the tears she's held tight flow freely. The statuesque beauty looks positively fragile in the man's arms.

"I hope he holds her forever," Kitt whispers.

Officer Monopoli steps close to Annie and speaks softly, "I'm Michael Monopoli."

She looks into the officer's eyes. "It's nice to formally meet you, Michael. Now, would you mind holding me? I've had a really bad night."

Mike gently brushes Annie's hair off her shoulders trailing his fingers along the silky strands. "It would be my pleasure, Sweet Annie." The young officer hugs her to him. She buries her face against his chest and shares her anguish.

Fred Serpico wheels Kittridge Mahoney off to one side of the hall and kneels in front of her. "Kittridge. Wrong place. Wrong time. But I'm seizing the day. I love you," he says as he brushes hair from her face and kisses her deeply.

When she can pull her next breath, she takes Fred's face between her hands and kisses him ever so softly, and asks, "Is it real love, faux love, or faux, faux, love, Detective Serpico?"

Fred laughs big.

Braving the night.

John steps out of the farmhouse with Callie and Tess. It is well past 2 AM. The girls overheard an earlier conversation that he had with Fred, and they insisted that he tell them what was happening with their mother and sister. Since then, none of them have been able to turn off the noise in their heads, so the three of them are leaving the farmhouse and heading to Mayflower-Falls Regional Medical Center. He reaches for the front door handle of his SUV, and freezes.

John's heart thumps an erratic beat because he knows—
Joy is back.

The End

More to come …

Please enjoy the teaser for my next book in the series, *Netti Barn* …

Netti Barn
THE MENACE

--- PULLING THREADS ---
Book Two
SHERYLL O'BRIEN

Where are you?
August

John Maxwell was passed out cold. His inert body slumped in a seat in the first-class section of a plane, "traveling at some godforsaken Mach-speed across the Atlantic Ocean." Those choice words were uttered during the last seconds of his lucidity. Unfortunately for John, and for his fellow passengers, this was the second trip, "across the fucking pond," he'd made in a handful of days. Despite his aversion to flying, on the first of every August he boards a plane, lashes himself to his seat, and sets about taking the edge off with as many whiskeys as allowed during flight time. When he's sufficiently liquored up, he suggests to everyone within listening distance, to not wake him, "should this fucking plane begin hurtling toward Earth."

John hadn't expected to be returning stateside so soon, in fact, he planned on putting at least 30 days between the torture trips, but there was no reason for him to stay in Madrid—without her.

Where are you?

His heavily encrypted message went unanswered each of the dozen times he sent it.

After spending five miserable days alone—confirming what he knew the minute he landed—that she wasn't going to meet him in Madrid, he packed up and booked a flight home, the one he was mercifully sleeping through. John Maxwell was about to find out that mercy sometimes comes with a price.

"Your turn," he nudged, as he tossed the final handful of A-Z alphabet letters onto their bed.

She pulled a piece of paper, and turned it his way. "I pulled M. You wanted M didn't you?"

He nodded.

"If you got it, where would we be going?" She moved across the bed, and settled into his embrace.

"Madrid."

"Why Madrid?"

"Well, I've never been to Spain…" he sang into her fruity-smelling hair.

She laughed that great laugh of hers, "Well, if you promise to sing that to me once every day while we are there, I'll choose Madrid."

He startled awake.

ABOUT THE AUTHOR

She is not dead.

Sheryll O'Brien crafts characters without constraints. She tells them who they are, then let's them show her better versions of themselves. She gives them life and they live it beyond her wildest dreams.

Sheryll is a lifelong resident of Worcester, Massachusetts, where she is wife to the most supportive husband ever, and mother of two adult daughters, one who refuses to leave her home and the other who refuses to tell her where she lives. Of most significance, she is MammyGrams to the sweetest six-year-old, Hadley.

Sheryll worked several years in the fundraising community of Worcester County, writing grants for non-profit organizations. She began writing for her own pleasure after surviving brain surgery and breast cancer. Happily, for her fanbase of family and friends—she is not dead.

If you have enjoyed reading my book, I would very much appreciate you taking a few minutes to write a review and post that review on amazon.com and goodreads.com.

The opinion of readers can help prospective readers make a purchasing decision.

To learn more, please visit my website, www.pullingthreadsnovella.com and subscribe to my blog for updates on future projects.

I would absolutely love to hear from my readers, you can email me at,

pullingthreadsnovella@gmail.com

www.ingramcontent.com/pod-product-compliance
Lightning Source LLC
Chambersburg PA
CBHW070825180626
46818CB00001B/397